Name: Mane Diane Pu

Phone: 301-263-0307

Address: 5009 Worthington Dr. Bethesda MD

The Lyon's Throne

"I would meet this Spaniard, if I had but the time or the inclination." She looks at Master White. "You may return with the girl to your house. I will see her again. The Spaniard will go to the Tower until I see fit to think upon his fate."

"But, but," I cry out, "you can't send Enrique to prison. He's done nothing, nothing at all!"

If I were twelve years old again, I might have stamped my foot like a petulant child. I fight the urge to pound my fists against a wall. My whole body is trembling as we're dismissed with a wave of the royal hand. Behind me, as I curtsey and walk away, Elizabeth's voice calls out in anger, "Your tongue is a whiplash, lady, and must be curbed. Not another word, or you'll rest in prison with your Spanish friend."

"Even readers who are unfamiliar with THE LYON'S ROAR will relish the continuing story that speculates on the fate of the settlers of the Lost Colony of Roanoke.... Even reluctant readers will keep turning the pages as they seek answers to the many questions raised. This is a fascinating glimpse at what might have happened to a group of people about whom little historical fiction is written."

—School Library Journal, August 1998

"Stainer does an amazing job of weaving fiction with fact, making this important historical event come alive in the minds of middle school students."

—KLIATT Reviews, September 1998

"M.L. Stainer has created a brilliant new series based on historical accounts... and a fervent imagination."

—Marilyn Walker, Cherry Valley Books

"The hardships the Roanoke colonists faced are depicted vividly.... The facts known about the colony are mixed well into the plots of the books, making for painless learning. The total effect of the LYON SAGA is a satisfying one."

—North Carolina Libraries, Fall 1998

"M.L. Stainer weaves fiction with fact as she explores the 400-year-old question mark in American history of what happened to the 117 lost colonists of 1587."

—The Daily News, Jacksonville, NC

Best Wishes!
M. L. Stainer

The Lyon's Throne

M.L. Stainer

Illustrated by James Melvin

GtG

James Melvin

Chicken Soup Press, Inc.

Circleville, New York

Chicken Soup Press, Inc.
P.O. Box 164
Circleville, NY 10919

Library of Congress Cataloging-in-Publication Data
Stainer, M.L., 1939-
The Lyon's throne / M.L. Stainer ; illustrated by James Melvin
p. cm. — (The Lyon saga ; bk. 4)
Sequel to The Lyon's pride.
Summary: After being rescued from a pirate ship, returned to England, and imprisoned at Queen Elizabeth's Court, Jess faces tests of loyalty to her Lumbee husband and to Roanoke Colony
ISBN 1-893337-01-4(alk. paper).
—ISBN 1-893337-02-2 (pbk. : alk. paper)
[1. Roanoke Colony Fiction. 2. Lumbee Indians Fiction.
3. Elizabeth I, Queen of England, 1533-1603 Fiction.
4. America--Discovery and exploration--English Fiction.
5. Indians of North America--North Carolina Fiction.]
I. Melvin, James, ill. II. Title.
III. Series: Stainer, M.L., 1939- Lyon saga ; bk. 4.
PZ7.S78255Lyt 1999
[Fic]—dc21   99-18190
                                                                          CIP

Book design by Netherfield Productions, Pine Bush, New York
Printed by Worzalla, Stevens Point, Wisconsin
10 9 8 7 6 5 4 3 2 1

In memory of Kathleen McFall,

a good friend who will always be in my heart.

Other Works by M.L. Stainer

The Lyon's Roar (1997)
The Lyon's Cub (1998)
The Lyon's Pride (1998)

Contents

Author's Note

The author wishes to note that some spellings of familiar names have been changed according to how they are listed on original documents.

Croatoan is pronounced Cro-ah-tu-WAN; Manteo, MAN-tee-o; Ananyas, An-na-NEE-yus; Akaiyan, Uh-KY-yun; Towaye, TOH-way; Caun-reha, Corn-RAY-hah; Rus-quauene, RUSS-kwor-een; Wauh-kuaene, WAH-kor-een; Quayah, KWAY-yah; Oohahn-ne, Oo-HAH-nay; Ooteinne, Oo-TEEN; Te-lah-tai, Tee-LAH-tay; Twah-ne, TWAH-nay; Cauhau-wean, Caw-HAW-ween.

A special note of thanks to:
Robert Peay and Greg MacAvoy for their proofreading assistance: to Stella Denton of Pine Bush High School library and Fran O'Gorman of Goshen library, for their help in research: to Ricardo Carballal for his invaluable assistance with Spanish: to Harry L. Thompson, Curator of the Port-o-Plymouth Museum, Plymouth, North Carolina, for his encouragement: to my mother, Harriet Stainer, and my friends and family for their continued support.

Tuskeruro dialect: from *A New Voyage to Carolina,* by John Lawson, edited by Hugh Talmadge Lefler. Copyright © 1967 by the University of North Carolina Press. Used by permission of the publisher.

i

Prologue

EVEN THOUGH THE Spanish Armada had been defeated by England, Spanish ships and pirate brigantines continued to forage the Western Ocean, making travel to the New World hazardous.

The English Court under Elizabeth I was a place of great intrigue, with spies everywhere. There were times Elizabeth wasn't sure who to trust.

It's entirely possible that news of Indians would have attracted the attention of the Queen. She had, after all, entertained both Manteo and Wanchese at her court.

It isn't hard to believe that Elizabeth would wish to meet another representative of such a group of "Noble Savages."

As Sir Walter Ralegh fell out of favor with his Queen, he sold the shares in his New World venture to various stock holders. By doing this, he hoped to guarantee continued exploration and fulfillment of his dream. Joint-stock companies grew in power, assuming a major role in New World exploration.

Chapter 1

The Pirate Ship

IT'S HARD TO REMEMBER everything which happened that fateful day in July, 1590. First, all was peace and happiness, then my world turned upside-down.

Akaiyan, Oohahn-ne and I, along with Enrique and Te-lah-tai, wait hidden in the deep woods outside our village. From the distance, I hear yells and screams. I want to run back to find Mother, my brother Thomas, now known as Cauhau-wean, to lead the *a hots* to safety, especially the foals. But Akaiyan's hand restrains me.

We're captured by the pirates who have landed on Croatoan Island. A small band creeps upon us in the woods, catching Enrique and Akaiyan by surprise. The pirates strip them of the bows and arrows, the *oosocke-nauh*, knives, even Enrique's firearm. They clout them about the head, but are gentler with Te-lah-tai and me. They even let me continue holding Oohahn-ne, my sweet babe. We're rounded up and herded down to the beach. There I see Carlos, Quayah and some of

1

the other unqua. Manteo, Towaye, Sinopa and some of the elders of the tribe aren't there. Neither is my dear Mother, nor my brother, nor other *nickreruroh*, English. I can only hope they're all safe.

"Master Bayley is dead," Carlos whispers to us. "And Manteo was wounded in the shoulder. I don't know about the others."

There's no time to weep, to question, as the rough men push us into their boats. One, I can see, is laden down with supplies stolen from us, our stores of food, the chest with coins from Roger Bayley's house.

What of the *a hots*, I think wildly, those sweet gentle horses that we love and who love us? What of their babes, Star, Hoonoch and Cotcoo-rea? Who will take care of them, now that all of us are being taken away? And where is Mother, oh, my dearest Mother? What's become of her?

As if in answer to my thoughts, Carlos whispers again,

"*Los caballos* are safe. They didn't want them, and Sooka is all right. Your mother and all the rest are well. They only want *los indios*, and those of us who look like *indios*, for sale or trade as slaves."

My heart stops beating in my chest! To be sold into slavery? The English part of me wants to cry out, "Wait, I'm *inglés*." But I say not a word, caution holding my tongue in check, for I can't be separated from my husband and child. I do all I can to keep Oohahn-ne from crying, to keep her warm and cradled against me. Tears fill my eyes as I remember Che-Chou, my little silver coat. He was shot down as he leaped to our defense, and his body now lies crumpled in the woodlands. Even an animal deserves an *unqua* prayer, so its spirit can find its way to heaven. I sit in the boat and silently mouth the words: 'May the little *squarrena* be at peace with

Oonaquera, the Great Spirit. May he find his way to the place of all souls.'

How can this all be happening? I sit in the middle of a rocking boat, next to Carlos and Te-lah-tai. My beloved Akaiyan and Enrique are in the boat following us. Te-lah-tai sobs and moans softly.

"Hush, hush," I whisper to her in Croatoan. "Don't make them look at you."

Indeed, I've seen the rough-whiskered men eyeing Te-lah-tai in a way I don't like. I'm terribly worried, for she's so beautiful. I glance over at Akaiyan and Enrique, who are watching us constantly. Oh, beloved, I think, what lies in store for us?

Carlos sits next to me, not saying a word. He waits for a moment when the pirates' attention is focused away from us and toward the high vessel we're approaching. As we near the shoals, the waters are rougher, the swells deeper. It takes all the men's strength to keep the boat from capsizing as up and down we go. All of a sudden, Carlos whispers, *"Adios,"* and hurls himself over the side. I start to call out, "No, don't!" but bite my tongue. The pirates don't seem to notice, so intent are they on working the oars and heading straight. I glance over the side, but don't see him. Oh, sweet Jesus, don't let him drown, don't let the men see him and shoot their weapons at him. Let him get safely back to shore.

A lump catches in my throat. Oh, Carlos, may God's loving hand guide your way. I turn once to look back at the shoreline of Croatoan receding in the distance. A mist lies over its far horizon. For a moment, I think I see Carlos' brown head bobbing in the waves behind us, the splash of an arm, the kick of a foot, then nothing! I can only hope and pray that he's strong enough to breach the waves and make his way back to

3

the beach. And once there he can see dear Mother, take care of her, tend the sweet *a hots* and grow in strength and resolve.

Perhaps one day we'll see each other again. Perhaps one day I'll return to this island home, to live in peace and breathe its sweet air once more. Oohahn-ne whimpers and sucks on my finger. A single tear traces its way down my cheek and with it, my hopes, my dreams, fall away.

Chapter 2

Enemy Flag

WE'VE BEEN SAILING north for many days now and with each new dawn, the miles increase between Croatoan and the pirate ship. The brigands who captured us suffered grievous losses from *unqua* arrows and *nickreruroh* firearms. Our losses, Carlos had whispered, were fewer; Roger Bayley died defending all, as did Master Hynde and Richard Shaberdge. Manteo and several warriors were wounded; we don't know how seriously. The pirates retreated under our fierce defense, and the small band which captured us in the woods joined with some who'd rounded up Quayah, Carlos and others. We were all quickly spirited away from the main fighting, back to a lonely and far part of the beach. The wounded pirates were left where they'd fallen, calling in vain for their comrades to rescue them.

My heart bleeds for them all, for Master Bayley who gave his life defending us, and for the rest whose fate I know not.

I sit in the bowels of this brigantine and think, once more

I'm a captive of the enemy, Spanish, pirate, it doesn't matter. All that matters is that the distance between my home and me grows larger and hope smaller.

The pirate flag flaps noisily in the wind above us whenever we're allowed on deck, which is usually once a day. The pirates don't want their profit to die on them so food, though barely palatable, is given on a regular basis. We women have been sequestered from the men. I only see Akaiyan and Enrique when up on deck, and they're at the far end of the ship at all times.

The wind rips the flag which flutters above us from its lofty height. What trickery, to deceive us so as they approached Croatoan Island, hauling down their fierce symbol to hoist aloft the Tudor Flag of our beloved Elizabeth. I try to remember stories that George Howe told me on our voyage over from England, stories of pirate ships which lured ships to their doom by flying a friendly flag. To think that we were fooled by such subterfuge!

We all need to bathe and a bucket is provided every third day for our common use. I've suckled Oohahn-ne in relative privacy, turning to the deepest corner of our quarters to do so. Te-lah-tai has stopped weeping, her face a mask of fear every time one of the men approaches. She keeps her head lowered as I've advised and looks away so as not to catch anyone's eye. I use rags to change my babe, then try to wash them clean after each use but no matter what, we're all beginning to offend each other. Finally the leader of the brigands, a man by the name of Calico Jack, calls for the hoses and they flush us with sea water. To provide us with some sort of privacy, a screen is rigged around one corner of the deck and the men not allowed to venture beyond a certain point. Reluctantly we remove our clothing and wash ourselves down under the showery spray.

It's not ideal but at least we feel clean again.

They still don't know that I'm not of the same blood as Te-lah-tai and the other women, for my skin's as dark as any Indian and I wear the shell and bead necklaces and dress in *ocques* clothing. I try to signal Akaiyan in any manner without drawing attention to myself. One day, when no one's looking, I manage to catch his eye from afar and blow him a kiss. He gives a brief nod of his head and I know he's seen me. It fills me with joy that he's still well and that none have seen us communicating.

These rough men speak a language all their own, not English nor Spanish, yet a strange combination of both. I can catch words here and there that are familiar but, for the most part, their dialect is unknown to me. The trip seems to have no ending, for as far as I can determine they're not headed for any country. Rather, they ride the sea lanes in this ship, the "Night Rambler," and look for others they can plunder. Whenever their supplies run low, they sail into a harbor which looks promising and seek sweet water and provisions. If that means raiding an *unqua* village, they do so with no qualms. If they see a ship upon the horizon, they rig their sails and head at breakneck speed to intercept, a flag of England, or France, or Portingall flying from the mast. As soon as they're within cannon range, down comes the one and up goes the fearsome flag. Already we've had two such encounters which kept us confined well below while the cannons sounded, and the defeated ship quickly surrendered and was boarded.

They rarely take prisoners from these captive vessels, for most in battle are killed immediately and the wounded are thrown overboard to feed the sharks, whether pirate or other. We're kept alive, we all know, because we're to be sold whenever they arrive at some place where there's profit to be made. How quickly they'll get rid of us, exchanging our lives for gold and silver coins the way Vicente Gonzaléz had. They watch us carefully, realizing now that they lost one, Carlos, before we'd even boarded. The men who rowed our small boat were severely whipped for losing him. They cursed and howled and their backs were raw for a week.

This Calico Jack has been eyeing Te-lah-tai with keen interest and I fear for her safety. Last night I spoke softly with her, then cut off her long hair with a piece of metal I'd managed to hide. She wept silently, the tears streaming from her big brown eyes. Then I took some buckskin torn from my skirt and bound her small breasts flat against her chest. The other *unqua* women are older and not as pretty. If he tries to take me, I'll kick and scratch his eyes out.

Chapter 3

"Careening"

THE SUN RISES and sets on an endless sea. A long time ago, my dear father told me not to be afraid of this Western Ocean for it was leading us toward the promise of a new life. Now it seems a cesspool from which we'll never escape.

Storms come and go, the vessel moans and tosses, the rogues swear and berate each other. The *unqua* wonder if it would be more a blessing to capsize and end it all. Only little Oohahn-ne keeps me from thinking such thoughts. In some strange code of honor, the black-bearded men don't bother me, leaving me private moments in which to nurse her, not making me an object of their lust.

Several times the captain and his quartermaster have come down and taken a couple of the women to pleasure themselves. Te-lah-tai has been most fortunate. Her chopped and ragged hair, her bound breasts, the dirt I've smeared upon her face, have made her less than desirable to them. They overlook her, taking instead two others who were married in our tribe. We weep for them each time they go, but they refuse to fight. It's something they must do in order to save themselves from certain death.

I see little of my husband and my friend. They and the other men are kept secluded, but they don't seem to be mistreated. A back scarred and bleeding won't fetch a good price at the marketplace.

My dreams are haunted by images of Croatoan Island, its sandy beaches, blue skies and brilliant flowers. I miss little Che-Chou, though grateful that Sooka is still alive, my mother's faithful companion as he sleeps at the foot of her bed.

And what of the *a hots*? I miss them the most. I miss their warm, earthy smell, their gentle ways, their soft noses and pleasant noises. I miss little Star, the first foal I ever saw born. I long to see Hoonoch and Cotcoo-rea. And I miss Beauty and Chaunoctay, Qui-heiratse and Utchar. Are Thunderer and Diablo still breathing fire at each other over the ladies? What wouldn't I give to see them all once more, to run and throw my arms about their necks, kissing their sweet faces, feeling their warm breath upon my hands! Qui-heiratse is in foal by Diablo. How can I not be there to witness the miracle of birth? I weep over and over at these sad thoughts, 'til my eyes must surely run out of tears.

Then one morn, the Night Rambler sails into the shallow waters off an unfamiliar coast. We're allowed to remain on deck, gladly breathing in the sweet land air. Suddenly, without warning, the ship scrapes bottom. She's run aground.

What possesses these sea-worthy men to run their ship into the sandy shoals? Surely they must know better? The boat and its cargo shift perilously to one side. The crates, cannons, and all of us slide to the port side, barely able to hold on.

Oohahn-ne begins to cry as I try to hush her fretting. The ship groans and shudders, canting to its left side, tilting heavily toward the waters. It creaks, then settles and lies still, its starboard hull exposed to the sunlight.

"We're shipwrecked," I tell Te-lah-tai and the others. "How is this happening?"

But the pirate rogues merely laugh while ignoring our concern. We watch as they fasten ropes to the ship and lower several small boats, rowing swiftly to shore. There, they run the ropes around nearby tree trunks and using pulleys, tug and pull upon the ship until it lists even more. The barnacle-encrusted hull stinks as the sun rises higher in the sky.

The men left on board clamber over the sides as some of the others row back. We can now see their purpose. With knives and shards of sharp metal, they scrape away at the barnacles, freeing the hull of its smelly burden. They labor for several hours until that side of the hull is clean. Then back they row to the shore, shifting the ropes and pulleys to the farther trees, tugging strenuously while those remaining use long poles to free the ship upon the waters. Then it's run aground again, only this time the port side is exposed. The process is repeated, taking all day for the entire hull to be scraped clean and daubed with tallow and sulphur to seal and waterproof.

I overhear one pirate explain that they do this at least three times a year to prevent the buildup of barnacles, which slow the passage of the ship through the water. It's also done to stop the infestation of the teredo worm, that tiny parasite which suckers itself to the hulls of ships, boring tiny holes through the planking.

During the second process the men row us to the shore, there to stretch our legs and glean what we can of supplies.

The men are made to gather firewood; some small game is hunted and killed for future use. The women are forced to gather nuts and berries. Calico Jack and his quartermaster take advantage of the shore time to lead the two women away. We watch as they leave, each of us grieving for their anguish, all of us knowing that should they ever return to their husbands, they'll be divorced as unclean and sullied by another man's touch.

Chapter 4

Ship Ahoy!

ONE DAY AS we languish below the decks, a loud cry assails our ears. We jump up, wondering what's happening.

"Ship ahoy!" the rogues call out, from the crow's nest all the way to the lower decks.

"Ship ahoy! What flag does it fly? Set the sails, full speed ahead, catch that wind, that's it, me beauty, swing our Rambler 'round. We'll catch her broadside and scoop her innards like a melon!"

No one comes to tell us anything but I know, all too well, that another battle will soon ensue. The Rambler groans in her effort to catch up with the other ship. Though a stout vessel, she's seen too many skirmishes not to feel the pain. Telah-tai grabs my hand and holds on tightly. Dear sweet Jesus, I think, will we survive yet another encounter? And what of my beloved husband? Will he and Enrique live if the cannons start firing?

We huddle in the darkness below, while the Rambler

catches each swell and sails hard toward her victim. What kind of ship is it? Does it carry the Spanish flag? If that's the case, we'll simply exchange one jailer for another. Could it be from Portingall or a French vessel? All these questions remain unanswered as we wait in the dark depths, holding our breath and saying many prayers.

We hear the shouts of the pirates as they call out to one another.

"Look out, mate, watch that rigging. Make fast the ropes, ready the cannons, get set to board 'er!"

I hear the sounds of cannon fire, that mighty "boom" which rends my ears. I brace myself for the impact of the ball, the smell of smoke and fire. Who'll fire first, the Rambler or the enemy? Who *is* the enemy? How can I tell here in this black hole of our prison?

It all happens so fast, I try to remember the events. We take several shots to our deck and our port side. The men are screaming, the cannons resounding. Then there's a sickening crunch and we shake from bow to stern. The two ships have breached each other's hulls. Smoke and fire are everywhere. I thank the Good Lord that we're not bound in chains to the walls as the ship begins to list badly. I gather the women together in a group, ready to make a dash for the deck before we sink beneath the waves. The Rambler has been badly hurt; the brigands are fighting hand to hand with the men from the other ship. It's impossible to tell who is who.

Suddenly Calico Jack appears before us, grabbing my hand and pulling me with him to the deck. He has a firearm and a cutlass. I clutch Oohahn-ne to my breast, keeping her little face covered as best I can. I can barely see through the smoke, except to notice the captain is now staggering upon his feet, a bloody hole where his face once was. Te-lah-tai screams and so do the others. Calico Jack falls at my feet and hands seize me from the back. I can't fight them off. Shielding Oohahn-ne as best I can, I feel myself pushed toward the edge of the ship. Am I to die in the depths of the sea? Oh, what will become of Oohahn-ne and me?

The hands pushing forward hold fast to me as I reach the edge of the deck. I'm swung around and find myself staring into Akaiyan's eyes. He draws me close for a single moment, then leads me onto the wooden plank which stretches between the brigantine and the other vessel. I get but a glance at the flags flying upon her mast and see the English banners whipping in the wind. A sob catches in my throat.

English hands reach out to me as I scurry across from the sinking pirate ship. Behind me is Akaiyan and behind him, I can hear Enrique, Te-lah-tai and other voices raised in fear. I want to turn to them and say that we're all right, we're on an English ship, but I'm quickly led to a place on the deck where stand all the prisoners, pirate and *unqua*. We're herded together and weapons are aimed at us.

The captain is a man called Richard Fendler. I want to run and throw my arms about his neck, thanking him for saving us. But I don't. For he's ordered his men to lock chains around our ankles and our hands. We're prodded below deck and into dank quarters. The only good thing is that the pirates who've survived are at the other end of the ship.

"They're going to eat us," whispers Te-lah-tai, her eyes full of tears.

"Don't be silly," I start to say, then I'm immediately sorry. For how would Te-lah-tai know otherwise? Those who aren't *unqua* have torn her from her only home, imprisoned her upon the sea, then died at the hands of other strangers who now hold her captive. What else can she possibly think?

Chapter 5

The English Captain

WE STAND BEFORE the English captain, Enrique and I, our hands still bound in chains. I can only imagine that he's noticed our blue eyes, so different from *unqua* brown, and wants to question us further. Oohahn-ne is with Te-lah-tai below deck, sleeping the peaceful sleep of innocence. He comes right to the point.

"You're not Indian? Then why in God's name are you dressed that way?"

I glance at Enrique, then decide to answer.

"I'm English and he's Spanish."

The captain and his men look surprised.

"An English girl and a Spaniard living among the Indians?"

"Yes. My parents are Arnold and Joyce Archarde. We sailed under the governorship of John White in 1587. Our destination was the Baye of Chesapeake, but we were abandoned upon Roanoak Island."

The captain nods.

"That expedition was deemed lost. John White has since returned to England and reported them missing."

My indignation can't contain itself.

"Indeed, we're not missing, but living on Croatoan Island with our friends, those of Manteo's tribe. And when did John White return to Roanoak?"

The captain smiles wryly, looking at his men.

"Your tone is arrogant, lass. Captain White reported to Her Majesty just before we, ourselves, set sail. He found no signs of the original colony. There was no distress cross."

I bite my lip. How can I explain to these English why we left Roanoak, that hostiles from the northlands were drawing closer to our encampment, that winter was fast approaching and the *unqua* offered hospitality.

"And what's become of all the others?"

"Half our colony set sail for the Baye of Chesapeake before that first winter. The other half went with the *unqua*."

"*Unqua?*"

"That's what the Indians call themselves."

The men stand around smiling.

"Savages are known only by that name, Savages."

"Indeed they're not, captain, but civilized and friendly."

He throws back his head and laughs.

"With painted symbols on their shoulders and shells around their necks like you. Civilized?"

I decide to ignore him and continue with my explanation.

"Those who went north to Chesapeake have since disappeared. When Ananyas went looking for them, he was killed."

"Ananyas? Ananyas Dare? I've heard of him. You say he was killed?"

I nod my head, fighting back tears. Even after all this

time, I think upon that news with such sadness as tears my heart.

"And what of the others?"

"Some decided to head inland and south. They thought they'd meet the Chesapeake colonists who'd left that area. Among them was Eleanor Dare, Ananyas's wife, and John White's daughter."

"Hmmm." The captain strokes his beard. "John White will be pleased to know that his daughter still lives."

I hope so, I think most fervently. I do, indeed, hope that fair Eleanor, little Virginia and my other friends have found sanctuary deep inland after all their travail.

"And what of him?" The captain points to Enrique.

"He's my friend, *mi amigo*," I say for Enrique's sake. "His name is Enrique de Gomara and he saved my life."

One of the captain's men reaches for his weapon.

"Spanish dog! Your kind killed my brother upon the high seas. Traitorous infidel!"

He rushes at Enrique, who manages to sidestep and avoid his knife. The captain snaps an order and the man stops short. He mutters something under his breath, but sheaths his *oosocke-nauh*.

"As you can plainly see, my brave men don't like the Spanish. Neither do I," he adds as an afterthought.

"Did England win against King Philip?" I ask boldly.

Again the captain laughs.

"Yes, in truth, we won. But Spanish ships and Spanish privateers still seek to plunder these seas. They're as bad as the pirates, if not worse. If you're English, then why do you dress like the Indians?"

"I'm married to the one they call Akaiyan. He is my husband. And the babe is our child."

19

"Half-breeds," I hear the men muttering one to the other. I can feel my face turning red with anger.

"An English girl married to a Savage? With a child? With a Spaniard for a... friend? What do your parents say?"

I think of my dear mother back on Croatoan Island, of my beloved father buried beneath the blue sky.

"We have their blessings," I whisper.

He laughs and pounds his fist upon the wooden table.

"Blessings, indeed. What will our good Queen say to all this?"

"Only take me back to Croatoan, kind captain," I entreat, "so I might see my mother and brother again."

"I think not," he answers. "We're headed back to England with our bounty. There the pirates will hang high from the gallows; there you can seek your own audience with our Queen. She's grown old during this war with Spain. Her temper is foul these days, I've heard. Take them away."

And as we're led out of his quarters, I hear him whisper to his first mate,

"Half-breeds, I spit on them. We should sell them for slaves at the marketplace."

Chapter 6

Voyage To England

IN SPITE OF the captain's animosity, we're treated more fairly than the pirates treated us. At least, they keep us together, and separate from the rogues who first captured us. Our chains are undone, for where would we run? I'm allowed to keep dearest Oohahn-ne with me, and Akaiyan is close by. The English have not taken our women for their sexual pleasure, and life is coming back into the faces of Twah-ne and Ooteinne. They both help me with my babe, washing her in the water provided in buckets, and crooning songs to her when she's fretful. Te-lah-tai's hair is beginning to grow back, much to her pleasure.

When Enrique first saw her ragged hair and dirty face, he couldn't believe his eyes. He buried his face on her shoulder and wept to think she might have been abused. But we all assured him that she hadn't even been touched. Twah-ne and Ooteinne turned their heads from Akaiyan and the others when they first saw them, for shame was marked upon them by the pirates' lust. But Akaiyan took their faces in his gentle hands, first one, then the other, and spoke words I wasn't privy to. They held themselves high after that and will deal with their husbands when and if that time ever comes.

Only Enrique is separated from us, for after his embrace with Te-lah-tai, the English sailors took him away and we heard he'd been chained on a deck below ours. To them, he's a Spanish traitor, the bitterness of Philip's attack on England still a festering wound. Sometimes I can overhear the sailors' whisperings, for they forget I'm English and speak in front of us in language of the roughest sort about their feelings against the Spaniards. But they haven't killed him and talk of a trial when we return to English shores. Perhaps it'll be a good thing, after all, for at that trial I'll happily testify on his behalf.

I've traveled now upon an English ship, a Spanish one, a pirate brigantine and now, an English man-of-war. It's a massive vessel and cuts the waters cleanly with its prow. Thomas, my dear brother, would have loved its cannons. I often wonder how he's doing back on Croatoan, as Cauhau-wean, an *unqua quottis*, or young man. I hope and say prayers everyday for young Carlos, that he made it safely back to shore and is, even now, comforting my mother and caring for the sweet *a hots*. It's now early in the year of Our Lord, 1591. My second child grows safely in my womb, as Oohahn-ne grows and will soon reach her first birthday. We've been upon the English vessel for well over a month as she plows her way back to England. My condition shows clearly to all, though I try to keep it as inconspicuous as possible. The babe within moves and kicks with vigor. I only hope we arrive on English soil before my birthing time. Ooteinne is carrying a child also, from the pirate captain. She tried unsuccessfully to abort it, but we stopped her. She wept and wailed, but we *unqua* women rallied around her, holding her hand and wiping away her tears. For a child is considered a blessing, even one resulting from lust. To end its life within the womb is considered an affront to the Great Spirit, a mortal sin in Christian doctrine. Ooteinne will deliver next summer, while my dear little one should arrive in early spring. I'm terribly sad at times, for dearest Mother won't be in attendance at this birth; there are no infant clothes to prepare for its coming.

So John White returned to Roanoak in August, 1590. And left almost immediately! Why didn't he sail his ship down to our island? We left the words "Croatoan" as a sign. And upon his return to England, he told our beloved Queen that we'd vanished without a trace! Captain Fendler told me that no ships had been allowed to sail prior to 1590. No wonder none came to look for us! Our much-needed supplies for that first winter must still lie gathering dust and mold in some forgotten warehouse. And now our original colony is scattered to the winds, some lost in Chesapeake, some inland, some of us still with Manteo's people on Croatoan Island.

It's up to me, I think resolutely, to go before the Virgin Queen and relate what has happened, to tell my story as best I can. I'm told she's fierce in temper and no longer moderate in her ways, that she turns her head away from the New World toward rising troubles at home. How will I entreat her to our cause once more? Will she even hold audience with me, dressed as I am in *ocques*, with an *unqua* husband and "half-breed" child? I could use my father's wisdom at a time like this, or good Ananyas's strength and resolve. How I miss them! I lie awake many nights wondering what to say, what to do. For to anger Elizabeth will bring ruin down upon our heads, and no hope of rescue for the English across the sea.

Chapter 7

Dockside

WE DOCK AT Portsmouth, that very same port from whence
I'd left over three years ago. The crossing is a rough one, with
winter storms continually besieging us and only the currents
of the Gulf Stream to ease our passage. When at last we weigh
anchor and the great ship settles in its mooring, I breathe a
sigh of relief.

The *unqua* are kept confined below as cargo is taken
from the holds. Shouts and cries are everywhere; the women
cringe with fear in spite of my assurances. Those assurances
belie the fear within my own heart. What if Captain Fendler
decides to sell us as servants at the great marketplace? And
what of dear Enrique, whom we haven't seen all these many
weeks? Will he remain with us, or be led away to prison?

Te-lah-tai turns her big eyes to me constantly, seeking
comfort and hope. I feel so much older though, in truth,
there's but two years difference in our ages. Ooteinne also is
my constant companion. She tells me stories that make my

blood curdle, that the English eat *unqua* babes for dinner, that Akaiyan and the other *quottis* will be drawn and quartered by massive *a hots*. Where she gets these stories from, I'm sure I don't know. Te-lah-tai listens with great fear.

When at last it's our turn to be led topside, the bright sunlight hurts my eyes. Smells and sounds assail my ears. Akaiyan and the others are bound in chains while we women remain free. I clutch little Oohahn-ne to my breast, whispering sweet words of comfort. But she's wide-eyed and curious at all the sights, and stares in amazement at the people jostling each other to catch a glimpse of us.

The men whisper among themselves. The women are more crass, laughing and pointing their fingers at me, at the men, at Oohahn-ne.

"Savages," they say derisively, though making sure to keep their distance. I want to stop and speak to them in the Queen's English, which is considerably better than theirs, stating my name and my parents' names. But caution holds my tongue in check. Let them think me a Savage, for all I care. I toss my head, holding it high and keep Oohahn-ne from reaching out her little hands.

"She's a proud 'un," one of them calls out. "Miss Princess, she thinks she is."

They all laugh loudly while my face burns red.

"Get along with you," Captain Fendler leads the way, pushing through the crowd of peasants with their dirty faces and hands. One of them reaches out to snatch the shell necklace from me.

"A trophy," she calls in a high voice. "See what I got!"

Akaiyan grunts and stills the woman's tongue with a look of pure fury. She gasps and her hand flies to her throat.

"Dirty Savage," she spits upon the ground. The rest of

25

them begin spitting and hurling things at us, mud and rotten food. Soon we're splattered with garbage. Ooteinne is crying and so is Te-lah-tai. But I refuse to do so, for that would give them great satisfaction.

"Over here."

Captain Fendler orders his men to lead us to a small tavern, where we're quartered in the back away from prying eyes. He takes pity on Oohahn-ne, who's now whimpering.

"Bring some water and rags to clean them."

That evening we're still at the same place, the only difference is that the noisy crowd has dispersed back to their homes. Somewhere an owl hoots. I look up and see the stars in the firmament, those same stars that shine upon Croatoan Island, I think. To my great dismay, my eyes fill with tears which fall unchecked.

They've given us some food, leftovers from their evening meals. Oohahn-ne is too fretful to take my breast and, besides, she's growing too big to suckle. Her teeth have come in and she hurts me. I take some food and feed her the partially-chewed meat. She eats well, then chews upon a crust of bread. I'm incredibly tired; the strain of the day and its derision having taken their toll. I lean my head against Akaiyan's chest and close my eyes. Oohahn-ne finishes her bread and grows sleepy. Soon we're all half-dozing, content just to be left alone.

How easy it would be to rise from my sleeping position, Oohahn-ne in my arms, take the women and flee. We could slip through the streets and back alleys until we were rid of this terrible place. But where would we go? Who in this bustling seaport would befriend us? And how could I bear to leave Akaiyan behind, my beloved who's still chained by his ankles to the others? How could Te-lah-tai leave Enrique, who holds her in his arms as they both sleep? What would the English captain do to our men if we were to escape? I give a great sigh. Akaiyan stirs and slips his arms over mine in an awkward embrace.

"Little Bird," he whispers, "I think the Great Spirit has deserted us."

I shake my head, putting a finger to his lips.

"No, don't say that. God is everywhere, watching over us. He'll deliver us from this place and guide us where He wants us to go. You must be patient."

He brushes my lips with a kiss.

"I'm not a warrior here," he sighs. "An *unqua* in chains. What would my father say?"

A sob catches in my throat. For Manteo, of all people besides my dear father, was the one I respected the most. I don't even know if he's still alive.

"He'd say to be strong and have courage. He'd say not to be *werricauna*, afraid."

Akaiyan looks first at the stars, then at me and our babe.

"He'd say to watch over my *kateocca* and my *woccanookne*...."

"And the one on the way," I add, feeling its kick against my ribs.

"Perhaps a son," he says grimly. "A son who will be born in this land of evil people, not in a place of peace."

Chapter 8

The Ride To London

WE'RE AWAKENED EARLY by the sounds of the English captain and his men coming for us. We're barely given time to stretch and take care of our needs before we're all mounted in a wooden cart drawn by six sturdy English horses.

The ride is long and arduous, but at least we're well rid of the townspeople. Several of them, those that were up at the dawn's light, follow us part way, jeering and yelling obscenities. Then we leave them behind for the trail over hills and across fields, through woodlands, until the horses are lathered with exhaustion.

The captain and three of his men ride alongside the tumbrel. After several hours, we stop to take refreshment and relieve ourselves. The women are allowed to stretch and walk part way into the woods. The men must take care of all necessities with an armed guard standing watch. Oohahn-ne is given food, as we all are, then a quick drink of water and back into the tumbrel again. Our journey continues like this for several more hours.

I'd forgotten how far Portsmouth was from London Town. We stop for the night at another tavern, sleeping once more in the raw open air. I try to cover Oohahn-ne as best I can, but it takes a while for her to feel warm enough to fall asleep. The tavern owner's wife takes pity on her crying and leads me into the barn where the horses are quartered. I feel terribly guilty resting there while my friends and my husband sleep outside. But soon Te-lah-tai and Ooteinne join us, then the other women. The guards make no complaint, so we throw clean straw over us and sleep a dreamless sleep.

The next morning, we're on our way again in what becomes a pattern for the next several days: traveling, stopping to rest for a while, traveling again, sleeping at whatever tavern is nearby. A wet snow falls constantly, dank and chill. We shiver against the cold. The captain has procured blankets for us to cover ourselves, for the nights are freezing. I overhear him tell one of his men that dead Savages are of no use, no profit, and his commission will be forfeit if he delivers a cargo of corpses. He comes to me one evening while we're eating the meager rations we've been given, signals me to give my babe to Te-lah-tai and seizes my hand, pulling me upright. I can sense Akaiyan's terrible rage, and only hope and pray he doesn't do anything rash.

"You're a headstrong lass. How did you ever get mixed up with these Savages?"

"They're my friends," I say stubbornly. "They helped us survive that first winter."

"But to marry one?" He pauses. "I can help you to get away. Just you," he adds, "and the other one carrying a child."

I shake my head.

"I won't leave them, not my husband, not the others."

He strikes me suddenly across the cheek. I gasp.

"You're a fool. These Savages are nothing to England, destined for the slave trade or worse, to be hanged with the pirates. Leave them and I'll provide sanctuary. I have a small place in Devonshire. You can deliver your bastard there and work for me. At least you'll have a roof over your head."

I refuse to rub my smarting cheek. The babe rises in my womb, thrusting a foot into my ribs. My hands go instinctively to cover my belly. The captain smiles.

"You're a comely wench. After your child is delivered, there are many... services you could provide."

He reaches out and touches a hand to my breast. I push him violently away.

"Never," I say between gritted teeth. "I'd rather die."

He turns abruptly, then stops and calls out over his shoulder.

"You'll get no further offer from me. The sooner I deliver you to London, the better."

"Captain," I say then, trying hard to hide the anger in my voice. "What will become of us and especially, of Enrique?"

"The Spaniard will be put on trial. Public opinion is high against traitors. The people will seek an execution."

"But... but... he's not guilty of any crime. He was pressed into servitude by his uncle. He...."

The captain waves his hand.

"None of that matters. Any Spaniard in London, indeed, in England, is still a traitor to those in high places. Hangings are what the people want to see."

"What of the rest of us?"

"A government official waits just outside London, there to take charge of you all."

He returns me to the others. Akaiyan has been gritting his teeth the whole time I've been away. He settles down only when he sees that I'm all right.

"Enrique's in danger," I whisper to him after the captain leaves. "They want to put him on trial."

"What does that mean?"

"They'll say he's an enemy because he's Spanish. They'll want to hang him."

Akaiyan grips my arms.

"What kind of people are these, that... hang a man. Enrique is *unqua* just like me, like you."

I shake my head.

"Not to the English," I say. "He's their *peor enemigo*, their worst enemy. It would go better for him if he were an *unqua*."

Chapter 9

John White

WE ARRIVE ON the outskirts of London by the end of the week, exhausted, sore and filthy. The tumbrel stops in the muddy street, and we're made to get out and pushed into a stone house set back from the road. The tumbrel drives on; only the captain and one man remain.

There's no food of any kind. Oohahn-ne cries and whimpers. I try to give comfort to her, but she turns her head away, her face streaked with tears. It breaks my heart to see her so; she was such a happy child before. Akaiyan and the others are kept apart in another room. I sit in a corner rocking Oohahnne, trying to interest her in a piece of ribbon, in her little doll that I've kept all the way from Croatoan. She plays briefly, then resumes whimpering.

Suddenly there's the loud sound of horses' neighing, the stomping of hooves, the rumble of wheels. Two coaches pull up in front of the house. We hear muffled voices, then the sound of footsteps. A man and his companion enter the room, wrapped in cloaks against the cold. The man speaks to Captain Fendler for several moments. Papers are exchanged, then money in large currencies. The captain nods in our direction.

"A wild bunch of Savages," he says. "I'm well rid of them, though what you want them for, I can't imagine."

He strides out the door with his man, giving me one last look. Not as well rid of me as I am of you, I think to myself, then turn to face our new jailer. The man rubs his hands together, shivering, then turns to his companion.

"We must get going," he says impatiently. "But first, food for them and warmer clothing."

The other man rushes out to the large coach, coming back with cloaks and blankets, some shoes, loaves of bread and strips of meat. He distributes all to the *unqua* while I stand aside, trying to puzzle the voice I've just heard, a voice familiar from the past.

"Eat," the man says, his speech still muffled from the wide scarf around his face. "Get them wine and water."

Te-lah-tai and the others shrink from him at first, then they grab the loaves, meat and drink. Akaiyan tears off a piece of bread and hands it to Oohahn-ne. He gives me some and then offers the rest to Ooteinne and Twah-ne. We all eat ravenously. Then we distribute the clothing. The man reaches deep into a pocket and pulls out the key to unlock the fetters around Akaiyan's ankles. When all are free from the chains, he stands to one side watching us curiously.

All this time I've said not a word, listening to this man's voice. Who is he? Who can he be? At last he speaks in garbled Spanish, his accent so pitiful I'd laugh under other circumstances.

"One of you is from *España*. I don't know who. *Los indios* all look the same."

I put a finger to my lips just as Enrique is about to reply. He catches my eye and gives an imperceptible nod, lowering his head and keeping quiet.

"It's all right," the man repeats. "You're safe."

Again I shake my head. This is a trick, I know it. The *unqua* stand quietly, bread still in their hands as the man speaks more urgently, this time in English.

"For God's sake, you must tell me. I've bought all of you at no small price. My last monies. When I heard of Indians brought back from the New World, I was compelled to leave my home in Ireland and...."

He unwraps the scarf from his face and I gasp. For I know this man, how well I know him! I last saw him kiss fair Eleanor upon the cheek, hold his new granddaughter in his arms, then turn and depart from our shores. That was over three years ago. And now he stands before me, John White himself, Governor of our Roanoak Colony, father of Eleanor Dare, his hands outstretched and beseeching.

"I must have news," he says. "One of you must know what's become of my friends, my dearest daughter, her husband and child? I'm a sick man, sick with grief. Say that my quest isn't in vain. Oh, doesn't one of you understand what I'm asking? Is there no one among you who speaks the English language?" I step forward, holding out one hand. He stares at me uncomprehending.

"You speak English?" he asks in a trembling voice.

I nod my head.

"Yes," I say. "Don't you remember me?"

He stares and stares, then shakes his head. How hard it must be for him, I think then, seeing an Indian woman with rounded belly, carrying another child in her arms, hearing her speak the Queen's good English. I smile at his strange expres-

sion.

"I look very *unqua*, don't I?"

"*Unqua?*"

"Indian. I look just like an Indian to you."

He nods his head slowly. "You don't speak like one. Who are you?"

"I'm Jess, Jessabel Archarde. Surely you remember now?"

"My God!" he exclaims, touching his heart. For a moment, I think he might faint with shock. But he quickly pulls himself together.

"You can't be little Jess."

"But I am. Only I've grown up. I'm married now to Akaiyan," and I point to my husband. "And I have a daughter, too, and another child on the way."

His companion fetches him a crate to sit upon, for there's no other furniture. He removes his cloak and puts his head in his hands. He's become an old man, much thinner and with graying hair.

"Jessabel?" he keeps repeating. "Arnold and Joyce's daughter?"

"Indeed, the very same."

He jumps up then and gives me a resounding kiss.

"And what of your dear mother and father? What of the others? I can't wait to hear the good news!"

Chapter 10

Where Is Eleanor?

JOHN WHITE'S COACHES carry us the rest of the way into London. We arrive at the house he has rented and are quickly ushered inside. It's obvious that Master White wishes no one to see us.

Oh, how London Town has changed since I've been away. New houses and stores have sprung up all over. Roads, newly-cobbled, twist this way and that. Smoke hangs like a shroud overhead; London is a city of industry now, breweries, soap factories, sugar refineries. We pass by the great Thames River, crowded with heavy barges, ferries and ships of all sizes. I've never seen so many vessels upon its waters. And what fashionable shops line its streets, bright with outfits of silk from China, furs from Russia, spices from the East Indies. I become very aware of my buckskin clothes, my simple shell and copper jewelry. My hair flows long on my shoulders, not fashionably coiffed in the latest rage. Vendors hawk their goods, each with his own patois to catch the ear. Te-lah-tai gazes at all with wide open eyes, as do Twah-ne and Ooteinne. Akaiyan and the others cast surly looks upon all they see.

"Tell me," John White entreats after we're properly settled in quarters that are small but comfortable. "Tell me all the news of my dear daughter and her husband and child. What of your parents? And that young man you were so enamored of, where is he? I've mortgaged my possessions to purchase your freedom. I've little left except my burning hope." He clutches his hands to his chest.

And so, I tell him all the events of our lives since he left us that long-ago August. It's hard to relate all the details, but I do the best I can. When I get to the part about Ananyas's death, he turns a ghostly white and I feel sure that he'll faint. His man-servant fetches spirits to bring the color back to his face.

"And what of my dear Eleanor? Where is she? Safe with your mother on Croatoan, I hope?"

But I shake my head sadly.

"Not dead?" His voice is a mere tremor.

"No," I say quickly, "but somewhere deep inland with Master Rufoote, Christopher Cooper, the Paynes. They hoped to meet up with George Howe and the others who left Chesapeake."

His hands go to his heart again. How sick with worry he must be!

"Are they safe?" he asks finally.

"As safe as any Christian soldiers can be," I reply, hearing my father's words echo in my mind, those very same words from long ago when I'd asked about George Howe at the Chesapeake.

"Was she well when you left her? And the babe?"

"Well, and looking forward to the end of her journey.

And little Virginia is now over three years old, a delightful child who laughs and smiles all the time."

"Aahh," he breathes a deep sigh of relief, then leans forward, clasping my hands in his.

"But how will she be found should I gain money for yet another voyage?"

"Oh, she's left markers scratched upon boulders with her own sweet hands. And they followed your original maps."

"Those maps," he shakes his head. "Just rough sketches based on hearsay and captured Spanish drawings."

On impulse, I give him a quick kiss upon the cheek.

"Dear Master White, thank you for your part in purchasing our release. But where will we go now? Can we get on a ship sailing back to the New World?"

He shakes his head.

"I've no money for your safe passage. And... and... the Spaniard with you... no ship's captain will take him on board. There's angry talk... about putting him on trial."

"But he's done nothing wrong, I assure you. He helped us escape from the garrison at Chesapeake. He gave us the *a hots*, horses."

John White stares at me.

"You've become an Indian maid, little Jess. What has caused such a change? Living with them, I suppose."

"They saved our lives through that first bitter winter. They shared their food with us, offered us hospitality, secured our safety from the wandering hostiles. Why shouldn't I join my heart and soul with them?"

He suddenly laughs.

"I remember that fiery spirit, how well I remember. But you tell me you're married to one of them?"

"My husband is Akaiyan, son of Manteo. My child sleeps

nearby. And I'll have another come next March."

He stares at my rounding belly, then shakes his head.

"Indeed, these are difficult times for us all. Tempers are high against anyone associated with Spain and Spanish things. There's great risk to remain in London."

I stand up, holding my head high and looking him straight in the eyes.

"I want an audience then, with our good Queen Elizabeth. I'll tell her of all that's happened since you left Roanoak. I'll tell her about Enrique and how good he is."

John White laughs and slaps his knee. Akaiyan stirs, then crouches ready to spring into action.

"It's all right," I whisper in Croatoan, putting my finger to my lips. And then, to Master White,

"Kind sir, I must insist, an audience with our Queen as soon as possible."

Chapter 11

Waiting

IT'S PLAIN THAT Master John White does not think seriously upon my idea of meeting with the Queen. He refuses to discuss my request and shakes his head, "No," whenever I broach the subject further. For the next several weeks we languish in his rental apartments while our fate remains uncertain.

The young men grow restless; they're used to hunting and the skills of survival. The women have no hearths to tend, no meals to cook. Twice a day, the man-servant brings bread, drink and some meat for us. Occasionally vegetables appear, not like the sweet yams and maize of Croatoan, but small soft potatoes and bruised carrots. We do the best we can with the little we receive. I entertain Oohahn-ne with songs and games while Akaiyan and the others talk about escape.

But to where? Somehow we'd need to get back to Portsmouth, enlist the aid of a sea captain, get on board and weigh anchor for the New World. And from what John White tells me, it would be well nigh impossible for Enrique. Poor Enrique chafes under the brand of *enemigo*, keeping very much to himself with only Te-lah-tai by his side.

Then one day, I'm summoned before John White in another part of his house. He tells me that soon I will change my clothes for those befitting a young English woman.

"For if you're to meet with our Queen, you must dress accordingly."

Such excitement swells within my breast.

"Am I to have an audience, then?"

He curtly nods his head.

"I'm working on such a meeting. But don't get your hopes up. She's not of good temper."

"I thought the war with Spain was ended?"

"The Armada was defeated but the war continues. Great animosity fuels our English hearts. Skirmishes upon the seas continue. We must take the steps one at a time."

Another week passes and I dare not say a word to my friends. For their talk is of revolt against our host. To hear me prattle about meeting some "unknown" Queen won't rest easily.

One late afternoon, I'm again summoned from the holding quarters. I quickly kiss Oohahn-ne, handing her to Ooteinne. I go to my husband and draw him close, unashamed in front of the others.

"I worry for you," he whispers in our language.

"I'm all right," I say. "Just a little tired."

He places his hand over my womb.

"Our child grows. You must rest."

"I want my son born at Croatoan," I reply. "I'll do whatever's necessary to insure our safe return."

Then I kiss him gently and leave.

To my great delight, I'm taken to a small room by a female servant, told to remove my buckskin and allowed to bathe. True, the water is tepid and the metal tub too small, but I luxuriate in the chance to be fresh and clean. Then proper English clothes are laid out for me: a simple chemise, a dress of homespun which hides my roundness, proper English shoes and a bonnet. The clothes are certainly not elegant, probably belonging to one of the women who works for Master White. As I dry and dress myself, I see the transition taking place from *unqua* to *nickreruroh*, from Indian to English. The female servant says nothing as she hands me a brush for my hair. She goes to take my buckskin garments, but I stop her.

"Please leave them."

She gasps to hear perfect English spoken from an Indian's lips. I give a smile.

"I was born in Somerset," I say, then no more time for the door opens and Master White's man-servant leads me down to the coach.

"Give them to my friends." I hand the clothes to the girl. "Tell them I'm all right."

She briefly nods her head.

During the ride to the Queen's palace, Master White quickly and efficiently tells me what to say. I'm not to anger Her Majesty who, through Her Divine Grace, has consented to meet with him and catch a glimpse of this strange half-English, half-Indian girl. I'm to nod my head, ask no special favors, let him do the talking and speak only when spoken to.

"I trust you understand?" he stares at me.

"Yes," I reply. "I won't embarrass you, Master White."

"Good," he says. "This was not an easy meeting to arrange."

I wonder briefly about the politics of the English court.

John White has told me that Sir Walter Ralegh is no longer in full favor with Elizabeth, his Roanoak Colony considered an abject failure. The Queen is fighting against bankruptcy, her coffers strained to the limit with all the charters she's awarded and the cost of battling Philip's Armada. Spanish silver from deposits in Peru has flooded Europe for many years and, accordingly, the value of bullion is depressed and prices high on all goods. I'm grateful that John White was able to buy our freedom, even at the cost of mortgaging his possessions. But we're stranded here in England, once my homeland but no longer. My heart beats wildly for a sweet island across the vast Western Ocean. I ache to see my beloved Mother once more, my brother, my friends and neighbors. I miss the dear *a hots* and little Sooka. The coach twists and turns through the narrow streets of London, then pulls up in front of an imposing edifice, while my eyes burn to fight back the tears.

Chapter 12

Gloriana

HOW FOOLISH I WAS to think that the Queen, Her Majesty, would see me immediately. To think that once I was ushered into that vast building, I'd wait only a few moments before being summoned. Surely in my child's mind, for I must still be a child to have thought this way, I envisioned the portals flung wide open, a man in full livery beckoning me, then an audience with royalty.

I sit drumming my fingers on a hard wooden bench, while John White confers with others who are also waiting. In truth, a whole gallery of expectant souls wait for their turn with Elizabeth, their few precious moments to plead a cause. They look as nervous as I, white-faced or else, perspiring profusely, mopping their brows and trying not to twitch.

We must have sat for at least three hours before she calls us. I'm having a hard time trying not to fall asleep, my lids heavy to keep open, my babe finally settled to rest inside my womb after tossing and turning most uncomfortably. I'm dozing, then a sudden sharp poke from Master White who is rising to follow the guard, beckoning me with his hands to follow him.

A large room opens before me and walking it, like a mile from threshold to the circle of her throne. There she sits in all her splendor, Majesty, Ruler of England, Virgin Queen, Gloriana, looking most uncomfortable herself in her high lace collar and heavily-powdered face. But what a face, devoid of any smile or humorous turn of the lip, stiff like a painted doll, framed in a wig of red hair, bejeweled with diamonds and other gems too numerous to mention! It's the face of an old woman trying to pass as young. And her eyes, I can't read them, cold and glittering like the jewels she wears. I find my legs trembling, my throat thick with wool.

"Your Majesty," bows John White, sweeping low to the floor. "I've brought the young woman you requested to see."

"Did I, indeed, Sir," she answers most imperiously. "I cannot remember ever 'requesting' such a visit."

"Nevertheless, Ma'am, she's here. Come forward, Jess, and curtsey to your Queen."

I don't know how to curtsey, never having been taught, never needing to know. I cross one leg in front of the other and give an awkward bob. I'm sure I can hear titters of laughter being smothered beneath hankies of lace. I straighten up, my face a flaming red.

"This is what you brought me, this... girl. But she's dressed in English clothes. I thought you said she lived with the Indians?"

"She did, Ma'am, but I thought it proper to have her dressed as befits your court."

Again, more titters. And I can understand why, my homespun outfit hardly more than a sackcloth compared to

the fancy ladies and gentlemen who surround the Queen, dressed in silks and satins.

"Never mind," frowns Gloriana, and the hushed laughter ceases. "Come, child, tell me your name?"

"I'm called Jess, Your Majesty."

"Your parents?"

"Arnold and Joyce Archarde, part of the original colony settled on Roanoak in 1587."

She frowns again.

"Ah, yes, Ralegh's misguided folly. They disappeared."

"Indeed not, Your Majesty, they split into two groups, one north to the Chesapeake and one south to Croatoan, there to live among the tribe of Manteo."

She silences me with a wave of her hand. John White is glaring at me.

"Aah, Manteo, I remember him. The Noble Savage."

"Yes, indeed, the father of my husband...."

"You're married to one?"

The entire group of courtiers gasp, while Master White is clearly fretting.

"Your Majesty," he intervenes, "you must forgive Jess. She's quite outspoken."

"And with child, I see."

She leans forward, peering at my rounded belly which, unfortunately, the dress doesn't hide at all.

I clasp my hands over the babe inside.

"You cannot hide it, child," Elizabeth says then, more softly. "But what possessed you... to marry a Savage?"

"They're not Savages," I retort, "but gentle people, loving and kind."

Her face grows hard again and I sense her anger. John White stands helplessly to one side, shaking his head.

"I can't control her words," he utters.

"Indeed, Sir, that appears to be true. But what of this... Spaniard... in the group. Who is he and what is his business in London?"

I start to speak but Master White glares at me.

"He is evidently part of their group, dressed like an Indian, also. He claims to be a friend."

The courtiers shake their heads and several of them begin muttering.

"Hold your tongues," Elizabeth snaps. She beckons me forward.

"Child, no Spaniard can be a friend to the English in these unhappy times."

"But Your Majesty he is, in truth, a dear friend, the one who saved me from the Spanish soldiers. He freed me and my husband and led us to safety."

"A trick, a trick," someone calls out. The Queen's frown deepens.

"I would meet this Spaniard, if I had but the time or the inclination." She looks at Master White. "You may return with the girl to your house. I will see her again. The Spaniard will go to the Tower until I see fit to think upon his fate."

"But, but," I cry out, "you can't send Enrique to prison. He's done nothing, nothing at all!"

If I were twelve years old again, I might have stamped my foot like a petulant child. I fight the urge to pound my fists against a wall. My whole body is trembling as we're dismissed with a wave of the royal hand. Behind me, as I curtsey and walk away, Elizabeth's voice calls out in anger,

"Your tongue is a whiplash, Lady, and must be curbed. Not another word, or you'll rest in prison with your Spanish friend."

Chapter 13

Enrique In Prison

ALL THE WAY back to his house, John White is silent. I can tell he's angry by the pinched corners of his mouth. He pulls upon his small moustache and drums his fingers upon his knee. I sit across from him, my face still red with shame and embarrassment. For I'd done exactly what I'd promised not to do, spoken out in angry words in front of Her Majesty, the Queen. Father would not have been proud of me. When at last the coach pulls up and we get ready to dismount, I ask him in a small voice,

"What will happen next, kind sir?"

"The soldiers will come for your friend and take him to the Tower. There, he'll wait upon Her Majesty's grace."

"How long...?"

"Who knows," he shrugs. "Elizabeth is a woman of many moods. One time she smiles and you could ask for anything; now she frowns and berates us all. You didn't do well today, young Jess. I'm afraid you only worsened your cause instead of bettering it."

I hang my head and walk behind him into the house. He dismisses me as summarily as did the Queen. I go to where Akaiyan and Oohahn-ne wait, where Enrique speaks to me in urgent Spanish.

"What of my fate, dear sister, am I to stay with you?"

I shake my head.

"No, Enrique. The Queen's sending soldiers to escort you to the Tower. There you'll have to wait until she sends for you."

He casts a fervent glance at Te-lah-tai, asleep with Oohahn-ne in her arms.

"What of my wife? What shall she do while I'm in prison?"

"She'll be safe here with us. Master White will try to arrange passage back to the Americas, I know, just as soon as he can."

Enrique takes my hand and pulls me into a corner.

"If... if I'm not to be freed, then you... must watch out for Te-lah-tai. She's with child."

"Oh, Enrique," I smile at him. "I'm happy for you."

"This isn't good timing," he says worriedly. "But the child is one we've waited for."

Akaiyan signals me over and I whisper to him all that's transpired. He frowns when I tell him of the Queen's anger and her decision to place Enrique in the Tower of London.

"What is this place?" he asks.

"A dreadful prison," I reply sadly. "But Enrique is not to be executed, just held until he can have an audience with the Queen."

"I do not understand your English laws. On Croatoan, if a man is found guilty, he's punished; if innocent, then he is free to live his life. There is no... imprisonment."

"We have to wait," I remind him. "Our fate is in Elizabeth's hands."

"And Enrique?"

"Te-lah-tai's going to have a babe."

"She told us."

"Perhaps that news will soften Elizabeth's heart."

We wait two more days. Soldiers from the Queen ride up and take Enrique away. Te-lah-tai cries and tries to go with him, but Akaiyan and the others hold her back. Enrique has no time to kiss her goodbye. We watch as he's led off and the coach pulls away. There's much sadness in all of us.

Whatever life we have continues as usual. Master White, seeing our anxiety, gives the *quottis* work to do which keeps them busy and focuses their restlessness. The *unqua* women and myself take turns playing with Oohahn-ne and trying not to cry. I've never realized how much Enrique means to me, what a big part he's played in my life since our escape from the Spanish garrison. He's become like a *caunotka*, brother. Te-lah-tai grieves as if he were already dead. She's begun keening the mourning songs. I go to her one afternoon.

"This isn't right," I say in Croatoan. "Your husband is very much alive. He wouldn't want you to be mourning him. Instead, you should be shouting with joy, for you carry his child within your womb. Do you want your child to be born with tears in its eyes?"

She listens to me as an older sister, and stops the mourning songs. She places my hand upon her belly, but nothing moves yet for it's too soon.

"In a little while," I say, sounding like Eleanor had sounded so long ago. "Feel my child. Soon yours will kick like that."

For indeed, my second pregnancy is coming to its end. It's almost March in the year of Our Lord 1591; the cold English winter will soon be over. I can smell spring in the air, though not the spring of Croatoan Island. My heart is heavy with longing for that sweet place. I wonder how dear Mother is doing, how Thomas grows to manhood. Will I ever see them again? Will I ever ride the *a hots* across the dunes and feel their warm breath blowing in my hands? I need to smell the salt breeze fresh from the sea and hear the sea birds calling. Such sadness fills my heart, for my son will not be born there after all, but here in this small house in the middle of a London I scarce remember, held captive by the whim of a Queen who rules with an iron hand, and worries about deceit and trickery at every turn.

Chapter 14

Half-Breed

THE DAYS, THE WEEKS pass slowly, inching along toward an unknown future. As we languish in John White's house, I remember Father's words to me so long ago as we sailed aboard the Red Lyon, our brave flagship. What excitement filled my heart that day leaning over the railing, watching its prow cut through the dark waters of the Western Ocean.

"Why do families leave all they know and sail upon these waters?"

"An imposing question, Jess," he replied, turning to look at me.

"We've left everything behind, our friends, our relatives, our homes...."

"To seek our fame and fortune," he laughed, then seeing my face, "Sir Walter Ralegh has paid a great price to outfit this ship and give us passage. He has a vision of greatness, to spread our English heritage to all corners of the known world."

"What do we know of this new world, Father?"

"We've his maps, his records and those of the brave men who crossed ahead of us. They say it's a land of rich forests and wondrous waterways, a land of immense opportunities. Sir Walter seeks gold, praise and glory, while we... we seek a new way of life and land granted to us by the Queen's Charter. It's a chance to be masters of our own fate."

How well I remember his words. Here in John White's house, we're anything but 'masters of our own fate.' What will become of us? What will become of us all?

Master White arranges for me, Ooteinne and Te-lah-tai to go to market with one of his older female servants. I relish the chance to leave these small quarters and breathe fresh air, see some of the sights of London Town. The woman's name is Anne Wimbley and she cautions us all to stay close, dress modestly and keep our eyes down. I wear the same homespun dress I wore to see the Queen; Te-lah-tai and Ooteinne have been loaned servants' garb, equally modest and drab. They take off their shell necklaces, their buckskin outfits reluctantly, winding their long hair in a coil under bonnets.

We ride in a small coach pulled by a single *a hots*. It's a pathetic creature, reminding me of poor Utchar when we first saw him, his bony ribs protruding. As we get closer to the market place, we see and hear the hawkers plying their goods, the myriad open stands of fruits, vegetables, bread, fish and meats. Chickens, ducks and geese in cages squawk, quack and honk their melancholy songs; dogs bark constantly. Both my friends shrink behind me.

"Stay close," Anne Wimbley cautions and I relay that message in Croatoan.

We're lost in a sea of people, a pushing, shoving mass of humanity. I can feel Te-lah-tai and Ooteinne clutching my dress, holding on as if for dear life. We follow Anne as she trots from one stall to the next purchasing produce for Master White's kitchen. She's obviously an experienced shopper and argues vigorously with each vendor, shaking her head when the price quoted is too high.

"What nonsense," she states firmly, her hands upon her broad hips. "My master won't pay such high prices for this rubbish."

Her shrewdness pays off in some good bargains, and soon we're loaded down with bundles and our baskets are full.

Just as we turn back to head where our horse is tethered, someone grabs the skirt of my dress and screams in my ear.

"Half-breed, you're a half-breed!"

I'm spun around to face a large bawdy woman, with round red cheeks and puffy eyes. She points an accusing finger in my face.

"Come quickly," says Anne Wimbley, angrily pushing the woman away. But the cry is rapidly picked up by others, "half-breeds, half-breeds!" A circle forms around us, blocking our path. Te-lah-tai begins to cry; Ooteinne huddles closely to me. Anne Wimbley pushes and shoves us through the circle, still heading in the direction of our coach.

"Out of my way, you louts!" she screams, wielding her basket like a weapon in front of her. The men and women fall back from her fury, but our passage is quickly blocked again. Someone throws dirt at us; a rotten potato hits Ooteinne in the face.

"Dirty *breed*!" a voice calls.

Suddenly I see the vicious crowd pushed aside; soldiers of the Queen shove people to the right and the left until a way is cleared for us. Te-lah-tai sobs against my shoulder. The soldiers hold back the crowd, whose anger subsides as quickly as it arose. We're suddenly standing alone in the center of the marketplace, surrounded by soldiers with weapons at the ready.

"Come," says Anne Wimbley and, nodding to the soldiers, pushes her way toward the coach.

"No, Missus," says one soldier with big ears that stick out. "We're taking 'em to the Queen."

"What?" she asks.

"The three wimmen come with us to the palace. You can go 'ome to your master's 'ouse."

"I'll do no such thing," says stout Anne Wimbley. "With me they came, and with me they'll go home."

"I think not," says big ears again, obviously in charge. "Come on," and he leads us to a coach drawn by six large *a hots* which I hadn't seen before.

"Tell Master White, please," I call after Mistress Wimbley, who's being escorted to her coach. She nods and then we're pushed into the carriage, the door slams shut and we're off to the Queen's residence. Te-lah-tai and Ooteinne both weep against each other, while I sit grim-faced. My back is beginning to ache me terribly and I tremble at what Her Majesty might want.

Chapter 15

A Royal Birth

HOW THE QUEEN'S soldiers knew where to find us, I'll never know. But I'm grateful for our rescue. Who knows what that ugly mob might have done to us, four women alone, though Anne Wimbley, God bless her, was surely capable of knocking a few heads about.

The ride back to the palace is a jostling one. The ache in my back is becoming more pronounced and I grit my teeth. Ooteinne and Te-lah-tai have stopped crying and are gazing in amazement at the building looming before us.

"What is it?" Te-lah-tai asks.

"The home of our good Queen Elizabeth."

Their mouths drop open as the coach pulls to a halt and we're summoned out. Guards escort us inside. Once again, we wait upon hard benches while Elizabeth takes her own sweet time in calling for us.

I strongly suspect that my labor pains are beginning, though there's not much I can do. Please sweet Jesus, I think, let this be over soon so I can return to Akaiyan and the bed where I've slept these many weeks.

I'm summoned alone to my audience with Her Majesty. This time I'm escorted into a smaller chamber. Unlike the throne room, it's warmer and more comforting, a woman's room, not a royal reception area. Gloriana sits upon a velvet chair. She's less imposing and more relaxed. There are no courtiers around, other than two ladies-in-waiting.

"Leave us," she commands and they exit, curtseying as they back from the room.

"Sit, child," says Elizabeth, pointing to a nearby chair. I sink gratefully into its plushness.

"You were in a dangerous situation," she comments, picking up a fan and waving it gently. I wonder how she learned of our predicament.

"Relax, my dear," she continues. "Here we are not Queen and subject, but two women chatting."

I find it hard to think of Her Majesty as only a woman. For she's our sovereign ruler, the Virgin Queen, God's anointed lieutenant here on earth. A wave of pain suddenly washes over me and I gasp.

"What is it?" she inquires, leaning forward. "Are you not comfortable?"

"Indeed, Your Majesty, I think... I do believe...."

A startled look crosses her face, then she claps her hands suddenly. The two ladies-in-waiting rush in.

"Summon the physician," Elizabeth orders. "And make ready this room for a birth."

What happens next is just a blur. Pain after pain assails me. I feel as if I might faint, but gentle hands assist me to the bed. There I'm made to lie down and what I remember most is Te-lah-tai's face and Ooteinne holding me. A male voice hov-

ers nearby and male hands take charge, pushing my *unqua*
friends to one side. I've no time to be embarrassed, no time to
long even for my dear mother far across the sea. I remember
calling for Akaiyan, "Oh, where is he?" Cold cloths wipe my
forehead, my face, while I'm wracked with the pangs of labor.
But God is surely most merciful, for the babe is in the right position this time and slips easily into the world.

"Push," commands the Queen's physician and I push,
one final aching push and then, blessed relief. I lie back
drenched in sweat, hearing the sweet cry of my babe.

"A fine male child, Majesty," says the physician's deep
voice. "A lusty infant."

"Let me see him," I hear her say, then slip into a deep
sleep. When I awake, all is dark and calm. My babe is no-
where near, but I'm not concerned. For I know, unlike Ooteinne, that the English don't eat *unqua* babes. Someone hears
me stirring and a cool hand takes mine.

"Rest," says a gentle voice. "You have a fine healthy
son. The Queen has placed him in his cradle. You've nothing
to fear."

Hours pass and dawn's light awakens me. I've slept the
sleep of one dead and long in his grave. I sit up suddenly,
looking around.

"My babe?"

"So, you're awake."

It's the Queen herself, sitting in her velvet chair. I can
see her dimly in the early light. She must have been there all
through the night.

"Your Majesty," I say weakly. "I'm so embarrassed...."

"For what?" she asks.

"To have... this infant in your room, your very own
room."

"My child," says Gloriana in a voice most soft and gentle. "True, I am a queen but underneath, always a woman, though my councillors would oft forget it. Too much lately have I been wrapped in the throes of intrigue, the passions of kings and countries. Last night all that ceased, and the only intrigue to concern me was whether you birthed a son or a daughter. I saw life come into this world, and it has touched my woman's heart."

Chapter 16

The Dream

"WOULD YOU LIKE some more wine?" the Queen asks, pouring the sweet red liquid.

"Yes, thank you."

We sit in a small anteroom, sipping warm mulled wine from a silver goblet.

"Have something to eat?" She offers me the plate.

"Why, thank you."

"You'd better not eat or drink until the food's tested. Someone might be trying to poison you. Call the official taster."

She claps her hands. For some strange reason, Akaiyan and Ananyas are sitting over in a corner, talking most earnestly. Somewhere I hear a babe's crying.

"There goes the child," remarks the Queen. She gets up, the room dissolves, and suddenly we're on the deck of the Red Lyon. The Queen is perched astride the large cannon in the center. Behind her, Thomas is waving at me.

"Lovely view," says the Queen, pointing to the rolling waves. "Have you met my friend, Lord Essex?"

The handsome figure of a young courtier drifts across my gaze. As I stare, the visage changes and I see Sir Walter Ralegh staring down at me.

"Not him," mutters Her Majesty, frowning. "He's lost an entire population of colonists. I'll have his head."

The babe's crying gets louder; the Queen floats off the cannon and comes to rest next to me.

"Never much liked children," she says, "noisy things crying and crying. Off with their heads!"

Ananyas comes over and picks up the screaming child in the Queen's arms. He hands it to Anne Wimbley, who promptly puts it into her large basket.

"Off to market," she says loudly. "Let's see what we can do with this one."

"Better get some good turnips," Ananyas orders. "We don't want any soft ones."

"Check his shoes," says the Queen. "Sometimes cryptic messages are hidden in hollow heels."

The babe is screaming louder than ever.

"Never mind," says Anne Wimbley, "I'll go without him," and she flings the basket over the side of the ship.

"No, wait!" I scream out. "Don't do that!"

I awaken with a start. All is dark around me. The babe crying is my son, whom I've named Caun-reha, lying in his cradle next to me. I reach over and gently rock him. The crying subsides.

What a strange and peculiar dream, I think, lying there in the darkness. The last time I had such a vivid dream was when we were taking Eleanor and the others deep inland. I remember it clearly; Ananyas riding the *a hots* up into the sky. I sit up in my bed and ponder the significance, but can find none.

I've been at the palace for almost seven months. My small room is near the servants' quarters. I've not seen Elizabeth since I gave birth and woke to find her sitting in the same chamber. Servants come and take good care of me, bringing me food and drink, clothes for my son and for me. But I've not seen Akaiyan these long months, and it's now October in the year of Our Lord, 1591.

I wonder how he's doing, if he understands why I'm here and he must remain at Master White's house. Te-lah-tai is allowed to visit on occasion, bringing me news of them all. Akaiyan paces the floor, she tells me, his eyes sunken and his mouth turned sullen. Ooteinne and Twah-ne play with Oohahn-ne, whom I've not seen, either. I cry when she tells me that, for I need my little girl as badly as she needs me. Te-lah-tai also says that no word has come about Enrique, still confined to the gloomy Tower; we both hold each other and weep with fear.

I tell Te-lah-tai of my strange dream. She puts her hands over her eyes, whispering and shaking her head. The *unqua* regard dreams as potent messages from those dwelling in the place where all souls go. But she can't tell me what the dream means.

"I do not like your Queen," she whispers in Croatoan, looking fearfully around. "For she has taken my dearest Enrique away from me, and kept you apart from Akaiyan."

Indeed, I'm beginning to wonder what ulterior motive moves the Virgin Queen to keep us all so separate. My babe grows and flourishes; my confinement after birthing ended a long time ago. Surely she'll release me back to John White's house. Surely she'll reveal her ultimate plans for the *unqua*.

Chapter 17

An Illicit Visit

THEN ONE DAY late in October, I'm made privy to some of the goings-on at court. The ladies-in-waiting are tittering and whispering, full of gossip. Even the servants can't hide their prattle. It seems that Sir Walter Ralegh has been disgraced, having gotten with child a Mistress Throckmorton, maid to the Queen. The fullness of her pregnancy can't be hidden any longer from Elizabeth.

The Queen's anger knows no bounds. She fumes and paces up and down, her councillors and courtiers trying to stay out of her way. Her temper rages and she lashes out at everyone, boxing the ears of any who even think to raise an eyebrow. How foolish, the servants say, that Sir Walter chose one of Her Majesty's ladies for his dalliances. It certainly was poor judgment, for did he not think Elizabeth would notice?

"Nothing 'scapes the royal eye," mutters Becky, one of the younger servants. "I'm glad it weren't me, that's certain."

"Is she very angry?" I ask timorously, thinking that this

will set us back further from any hopes of returning home.

"Anger ain't the word fer it. She curses like a man, she does, and threatens to send 'im to the Tower."

"But Sir Walter's her favorite."

"Not for a long time," says Becky firmly. "She's 'ad 'er eye on young Essex. You mark me words, Sir Walter's days are numbered."

I've begun biting my fingernails, a terrible habit. But I'm so nervous, so lonely without Akaiyan. I long to see sweet Oohahn-ne. Akaiyan hasn't even seen his son. I speak in hushed whispers to Te-lah-tai and present my plan to Becky. She's the only one I can trust.

So one late afternoon, Te-lah-tai goes back to John White's house carrying a message. If at all possible, I'll come to visit my friends, bringing Caun-reha with me. My heart races at the dangerous thought of defying Her Majesty. But I must see my husband and daughter.

The opportunity presents itself within a few days. Elizabeth is engaged with her Privy Council, conferring behind closed doors. She sits in her small office signing document after document, talking with her ministers. Becky has arranged for me to slip out of the palace with Te-lah-tai, dressed in a servant's garb and carrying my son in a basket. It will appear as if we're to do shopping at the market. Instead, the small coach will drive to John White's house, where I can spend an hour or so with my beloved husband and my dear friends.

It's a risky plan, for to anger Elizabeth will set back my cause. But a mother's love is too strong to deny. I dress quickly, with trembling fingers trying to button my bodice. Becky tucks Caun-reha into the basket, covering him with cloths to appear like a bundle. I've fed him and given him a biscuit to chew on. I can only hope and pray he won't cry and alert the guards.

All goes according to plan. The guards don't even question us as we enter the small carriage. They're used to seeing Te-lah-tai and the servants coming and going. The horse pulls away and soon the palace disappears behind us. I lean back in the coach, flush with the thought of soon seeing Akaiyan.

I can remember it as clearly as yesterday. Akaiyan rushes out, pulling me and our son inside the house. My friends surround me joyously, hugging and taking turns holding Caun-reha. Ooteinne comes with her child born in July, a girl called Au-hoorah. Akaiyan's eyes are full of tears when he sees his son. He leans over and kisses him, then turns to hold me tightly. Oohahn-ne comes running and I gasp. For my daughter is now over a year and a half old, walking, running, clapping her hands. At first, she hangs back shyly, for she hasn't seen me in so long. Then she throws her arms about me and calls my name over and over. I bury my face in her hair and sob uncontrollably. Sweet Oohahn-ne looks just like my dear mother.

Then Akaiyan hands Oohahn-ne and Caun-reha to Te-lah-tai and Ooteinne, and leads me to a small private room. There he holds me close, tenderly caressing me, speaking sweet words of love and intimacy. He pulls me down upon a small mattress and we kiss, embracing each other with a forgotten passion.

I return to the palace with great reluctance, only doing so because I must keep Elizabeth's trust. It's hard to break away from my friends' outstretched arms, hard to see them cry with longing. Akaiyan has held me and loved me, so that must indeed sustain me for the weeks to come. He kisses Caun-reha once more and holds him high.

"My son will be a warrior," he says, his voice choking.

"One day, he'll be free to hunt and roam the woodlands."
Then he turns to me.

"I know you, Little Bird, only too well. What is the English name you have given him?"

"William Arnold," I reply, taking Caun-reha from his arms. "It's a noble name."

"It's an English name," Akaiyan says through gritted teeth. "And they are my enemy for keeping me from my people."

I leave him then, returning to the small coach which leads us once again through the winding streets of London, back to the Queen's palace, back to the Queen's prison.

Chapter 18

To The Tower

THOUGHTS OF AKAIYAN sustain me over the next few days, his gentle hands, his warm lips, the deep dark beauty of his smile. I grow sad when I remember the pain on his face at our leaving, how he held Caun-reha aloft then kissed the babe's cheek. I think of little Oohahn-ne who cried when I had to go, throwing her arms about me and clinging to my skirt. Ooteinne began to sing an *unqua* song to distract her, and she turned and started clapping her little hands together.

I wept all the way back to the palace, tears which wouldn't stop. Te-lah-tai cried also, for me, for her, now beginning her eighth month of pregnancy, for Enrique whose fate is unknown to all of us.

In the middle of my memories one afternoon, Gloriana herself sweeps into my chamber, bringing an entourage of courtiers in her wake. I can hear them approaching, like a wind soughing in the trees before a big storm.

"Come," says Elizabeth, clapping her hands imperiously. "Leave the child with the servants. You, also," she nods curtly at Te-lah-tai. My dear friend shrinks behind me, afraid of this *nickreruroh* queen who may yet devour her!

We trot dutifully behind the Queen down the broad sweeping lawns to the riverside, there entering a small vessel which rows us steadfastly to that imposing structure, the Tower of London. From the river we climb the steps to the fortress, passing through Traitor's Gate and into a world of gloom. What a dismal place it is! The bricks are old; some look in a state of decay. The guards come swiftly to attention as the Queen mounts the stairs. Like the whirlwind she is, she sweeps us into the dark Tower, climbing endlessly until we reach the cell wherein Enrique has languished these many months.

Te-lah-tai is breathless from the climb, holding her swollen belly and grimacing. But Gloriana doesn't seem to notice or care. The guard unbolts the door; it creaks open slowly and we enter, stooping a little and standing still until our eyes adjust to the gloom.

Enrique comes forward to see who it is. At least he isn't chained to the walls. He muffles a cry when he sees me and Te-lah-tai, them remembers the royal figure and bows low. He is thin and appears wasted. I wonder what they've been feeding him.

"Can you speak English?" Elizabeth demands in her royal voice.

"Yes," he replies slowly, "though not as *perfecto* as I'd like."

"Good enough," she nods her head. "Your wife and friend are here to see you. I shall wait outside."

Amazingly she turns and withdraws, leaving the three of us alone. Te-lah-tai rushes into Enrique's arms. He smothers

her with kisses as she weeps uncontrollably.

"Dearest Te-lah," he whispers. "How I've missed you. And so large with our child."

He turns to me.

"Little sister," he pulls me close. "How is your child? I don't know even if it's a son or a daughter."

"A fine son," I say, smiling and crying at the same time. "He's almost seven months old."

"And Te-lah, when will her babe come?"

"Another month," I answer, stepping back. I'm embarrassed to be there as they hug and kiss each other, remembering my special moments with Akaiyan. But Enrique holds out his hand to me.

"Stay by her side, sweet Jess, dear sister, for if I can't be there, you must...."

"I will, I will."

"I'd almost given up hope of ever seeing you again."

He's lapsed into our now familiar patois, a blend of Spanish, Croatoan and some English words thrown in for good measure, when we can't find the exact meaning in either language. I hug him and stroke his bearded face. His hair is dirty and unkempt, his flesh weak, but his eyes still shine with the fire in his Spanish soul.

"Don't give up hope," I whisper, remembering the Biblical words from Jonas, swallowed whole in the whale's belly, "...ascribe the cause of thy deliverance unto the mercy of God." Then I kiss him gently on the lips. "We will yet find a way to save you."

Elizabeth enters the room.

"We must leave," she commands, her keen eye noting our embraces, our smiles for each other. "There's talk of a trial, my councillors are insisting."

She sees our faces and her voice softens just a little. "But I will see justice prevail."

And we're swept from the cell as swiftly as we entered. I hold Te-lah-tai's hand and pull her down the steps behind me, an easier progression than our ascent. She bites her lip to stop crying and squeezes my hand tightly. A strange feeling stirs suddenly in my breast, a strange hope which flutters there like a sweet bird waking in its nest. Flutter, flutter, first one wing, then the other as it stretches to test balance and leverage. A trial, justice to prevail, this unexpected visit, what can it mean? Dare I nurture this small bird further?

Chapter 19

Trial Preparations

THE DAYS PASS in a torrent of activity. The Queen attends meeting after meeting with her Privy Council, the whole palace bustling with noise. I haven't seen her for days since we visited with Enrique. It's almost as if that clandestine meeting never occurred. Te-lah-tai's time draws closer and closer; the babe has dropped in her womb and her birthing hour is near.

The maid-servant, Becky, is my eyes and ears to any gossip. Sir Walter's been banned temporarily from court, clearly in disfavor. Mistress Throckmorton is confined to quarters and weeps a lot. There's news of a trial for some Spaniard in the Tower, Becky says rather gleefully, while my heart sinks with trepidation. Then she sees my face.

"Oh Lordy, Mistress, is that your friend? A Spannard?"

I nod my head.

"He's no enemy, Becky," I state firmly. "He rescued us from Spanish *soldados*. He's a peace-loving man, a farmer at heart."

She shakes her head.

"There's talk 'o swift justice, there is. Off with 'is 'ead, some say. Imagine, a friendly Spannard...?"

"All things are possible," I remind her, yet my hands are trembling. "And what of the Queen's disposition these days?"

"Just yesserday, she 'ad a fit 'o temper with her favorite, Essex." Becky giggles. "Can't imagine them two as lovers, now can ye?"

But courtly amours don't fill me with glee like poor Becky. That's all she has to consume her time, which is little enough after cleaning, sweeping and fetching for all the fine satined ladies. I'm only concerned that Elizabeth's last words spoken in the Tower won't be forgotten, "But I will see justice prevail." Will it be justice for England, I wonder, to hang an enemy high on the gibbet? Or justice for Enrique, wrongfully imprisoned for the crime of being Spanish?

Te-lah-tai goes into labor and delivers quickly. A fine boy child is birthed, giving lusty cries to all within earshot. She has an easy time of it, for which I give great thanks. When I go to see her, tears stream down her face. Whether they're from joy at having a son, or worry over Enrique, I don't rightly know.

"I shall name him Rus-quauene," she says weakly, "but Enrique will think of a fitting Spanish name when all this is over and we're back on Croatoan." The tears roll down her cheeks.

"Will that ever happen?"

"Indeed it will," I say, grasping her hand tightly. "For the Queen has promised justice for Enrique, and she'll keep her word."

John White pays me several visits and tells me that Enrique's name is on the docket for a trial. The prosecutors are drafting the charges.

"And who will defend him?"

He shakes his head sadly.

"Indeed, I don't know."

"Perhaps you, dear Master White. For you know his good intent."

"I know only what you've told me, little Jess, nothing more. That won't hold up in an English court of law."

"Then I must see the Queen again," I say with fierce determination.

He shakes his head again, a pained expression on his face.

"Your child's heart thinks it can demand an audience with Her Majesty whenever it likes. You're here by her good graces, nothing more. You mustn't anger her further."

"I'm not afraid."

"You know so little of worldly ways. This court is a hotbed of intrigue. Just think, she respects and admires Sir Walter, and still she doesn't hesitate to banish him from court."

"I don't care," I say stubbornly, rocking Caun-reha until he falls asleep in my arms. "I can't let anything happen to Enrique, I won't...."

My audience with Elizabeth comes two days later, when I'm summoned unexpectedly to her small private chamber.

"It is time to send you and your... friends away from London."

"Away where?"

She stares at me, her eyes hard.

"I said your tongue was a whiplash, Lady. It has not improved with the passage of time."

"Your Majesty, oh, dear Majesty, forgive me. I know nothing of courtly manners. My beloved father was but a carpenter, building houses in the New World for the glory of England. We've been swept from our homes across the Western Ocean through no fault of our own. I beg you to forgive me."

I kneel down in front of her, my cheek wet with tears.

"Child," she raises my chin with her hand. "Child, weep not. You will not be harmed, you have my word. I have arranged passage on a merchant ship back across the seas. Is that not what you wish for most of all?"

"All of us?"

She frowns.

"For you and your Indian friends."

"For Enrique, who has done no wrong?"

She purses her lips. For a long time she says nothing. Finally she rises.

"My councillors are insisting on trying this young man. Fever against Spain still runs high."

"But Your Majesty, he's done nothing...."

She looks down at her pale hands bedecked with jewels of ruby and diamond, which I've never seen nor ever will again.

"My hands are tied," she says wearily. "A Queen is oft but a puppet pulled by strings. My personal will is transcended by law. Loyal subjects, 'enemies,' blend into one; everywhere I turn are roosters all, crowing loudly, strutting this court as if it were a barnyard." She stares at me for a long time.

"Go back to your New World, to your happiness, your Noble Savages. You are the lucky one, if you had but the good sense to see."

Chapter 20

Back To Portsmouth

WITHIN TWO WEEKS, we're packed and ready to depart. Te-lah-tai is still recovering from birthing. With Ooteinne's daughter, our little band has now increased by three.

"But we've lost one," I weep, holding Caun-reha. He doesn't understand, of course, but gurgles delightedly while pulling on my hair. John White has given us supplies to fortify us during our journey back to Portsmouth. He tells me our safe passage has been purchased by the Queen's minister himself, Lord Burghley.

We remain at Master White's house waiting for the coaches to come and transport us. I'm not sorry to leave London, for its pulse and hectic pace beat a discordant rhythm in my veins. I'm definitely more *unqua* than *nickreruroh*; Mother was right all along. I can turn my face away from my English roots and look toward the western horizon. For beyond the vast sea and the setting sun lies my home and my heart.

Akaiyan gathers me in his arms, kissing Caun-reha

while I hug Oohahn-ne with equal passion. I marvel at Ooteinne's little girl-child while she, in turn, kisses Te-lah-tai and
her babe. But beneath our joy at being reunited, at knowing
we're going home, lies the dark grief of leaving Enrique behind. For his future is one of almost certain death. Te-lah-tai
is frantic, looking first to me, then to John White, as if to seek
answers neither of us can give. When the coaches pull up and
the time comes for us to embark, she screams and runs into
the farthest room, huddling in a corner. It takes Akaiyan and
two others to pull her to her feet but even then, she refuses to
move. Only when Akaiyan hands her babe to Twah-ne and we
turn to leave, does she run after us. We enter the carriages in
great sadness, the women weeping, the men with sullen, stoic
faces.

I've said my goodbyes to Master White, who must remain
behind. He tells me he's soon to be moving from London back
to his home in Newtown, Ireland, in the fair county of Cork.
There will he live the rest of his days, "a simpler life than this
one has been," he says wryly. His face is lined and creased
with worry over Eleanor and little Virginia. I've promised to
do all I can to find out anything, where they are, if they're well
and happy. He, too, has promised to do his best to return some
day.

The coaches carry us swiftly mile after mile; the shroud
of smoke and gloom above London disappears until the only
grey overhead are the clouds of a December sky. I know in my
heart it's not the best time for crossing the ocean; winter
storms can wreak havoc on ships and ice choke the sea lanes.
But it's also a good time, for pirates and their kind don't ply
the seas during these months, preferring instead to languish
in warmer ports. I shall pray for reasonable weather and a
speedy voyage.

A deep sorrow pervades me. I haven't seen Elizabeth since our last meeting. Papers have been given to me by John White signed, he says, by Lord Burghley and with the Queen's seal. I wish he were with us now, to see us safely aboard a sturdy vessel. I close my eyes, trying to get some rest before we reach our final destination.

When at length we arrive at Portsmouth, we're scarcely given a look. Unlike last time, wind and snow whip around us affording protection from hostile stares. We huddle together until a seaman comes and asks for my papers. I hand them to him and he leads our group to the dock, alongside a massive merchant vessel. It has several large cannons. Goods and all manner of cargo are being hoisted aboard. We're made to wait over an hour until once more, the seaman leads us on board. We're led below deck and assigned a small space. This will be our home upon the seas.

We eat a little of the food left over from our journey. The babes are tired and hungry. They cry fretfully and the sound fills the small space and echoes round and round the planked walls. We try to hush them, singing all manner of *unqua* songs until they finally fall asleep. All of us are exhausted from the journey. There was no time to say goodbye to our escort, Master White's man-servant. He just nodded his head curtly and turned to leave, mounting a coach alongside the driver. Goodbyes are often like that, abrupt and somber. And sometimes, I think, there's no time to say goodbye at all.

I drift off into a restless sleep, dreaming of Gloriana sitting upon her throne dictating English law, boxing the ears of her ministers. Then the image shifts and a different woman appears, one softer and more feminine, holding a sleeping child in her arms. The image shifts again and before me is the shadow of a gallows, with a swinging figure upon it. 'Enrique,'

I start to call out, 'is that you?' I awake with a start to feel the pitching motion of the great merchant vessel. We're pulling out of Portsmouth Harbor, heading through the channel toward the outer seas.

"What a strange dream," I whisper to Akaiyan in Croatoan. "I thought I heard Enrique's voice calling me."

"You did," he whispers back, a faint smile upon his lips. And out of the shadows comes one I thought I'd never see again, my dear friend, swathed in a dark cloak which covers all but his shining eyes.

"Enrique, is that you?"

"Yes, my little sister. *El es tu hermano*, I am here with you and we're all going home."

Chapter 21

Clandestine Departure

ENRIQUE TELLS US all that's happened since we last saw him. For a long time his heart was full of despair, for having seen Te-lah-tai and me his hopes had risen then were swiftly dashed when no news came. He was treated no differently, neither fairly nor unfairly. Meager rations were still brought; the rats still played in the walls, coming out at night with eyes gleaming and whiskers tickling as they ran across his legs. From his small window he watched the sky, saw the snow when it fell, felt the cold bite of winter. Only a thin blanket was given him and that, barely enough to keep from freezing.

"I passed the day remembering my Croatoan, and the English words and phrases. I recited poetry and songs from my childhood; I even made up some poetry." He glances at Te-lah-tai who's beside herself with joy.

"Rus-quauene is a good name," he tells her. "But what does it mean?"

"Beaver-king," she replies solemnly.

"Beaver? Why not lion or bear?"

"I like the name," she pouts, then immediately begins to smile. "But if you wish to change it, dear husband...."

"Most definitely," he murmurs, but seeing her face, "we can call him that until I can think of a good Spanish name."

"You'd be safer with an *unqua* name for now," I caution him. "Who spirited you on board?"

"I don't know. I was sleeping in the cell when the door opened. An unknown guard came in, one I hadn't seen before. He tied my hands in front of me and pointed his weapon, and we slipped out quietly. There were no others around. The night was dark. I thought perhaps he was going to kill me. But two *caballos* waited in the trees and we mounted, riding hard and fast for days, it seemed. We rested but a short time before we rode again. I recognized this seaport from when we'd landed. Just before dawn he gave some papers and coins to a sailor and I was led on board. I've been waiting here for several hours. When at last I saw you entering, I knew I was being spared. But under whose orders, I don't know."

I stare at my friend sitting next to his wife and child and a warmth spreads slowly through my chilled body, like the glow I felt after Father once let me sip red wine at a holiday. A gladness fills my heart and my spirit sings. For I know whose orders freed Enrique. How well I can picture the scene, the small private chamber with no prying eyes to witness, the signature stroked boldly, the melted wax stamped with the royal seal in great deliberation; finally the steadfast hand passing it to her trusted Burghley. Elizabeth, Gloriana, Virgin Queen, a woman who longs for love but scorns the fawning of her courtiers, a woman who recognizes true friendship when all about her are filled with duplicity and deceit, this is the Queen I'll always remember. I pray to God for her good health. The merchant vessel plows steadily through the channel leading to the great sea. No one has come below to see us, but in a corner are food supplies and a keg of drinking water. The coins have paid our passage; the Queen's seal has assured our safety. Rough pallets are piled in another corner and we arrange ourselves as comfortably as we can. The air is dank but a small breeze comes through the slatted door.

I can think of nothing else but going home. Akaiyan's dour expression has lifted and he talks of seeing Manteo again and Quayah, his brother. Enrique can't believe his good fortune. He kisses Te-lah-tai unashamedly and with great abandon, not caring who sees him.

Our quarters are filled with babes' cries and *unqua* songs. Oohahn-ne is fascinated with her younger brother and sits for hours playing with him. She's almost two, which I find hard to believe. Caun-reha is starting to toddle around. Barely nine months old, he holds on to anything that doesn't move and explores our small surroundings.

I pray for fair weather and smooth sailing, though I know that we'll probably have neither. For December rounds into January in the year of Our Lord, 1592. I'm now nineteen and Thomas, back home, will have turned sixteen. I'm nineteen, married, with two small children and an *unqua* husband. I wonder what dear Mother will say when she sees us all again. I wonder what Eleanor would think if she knew of my husband and babes. How is little Virginia doing? Are they well and happy? I make a solemn promise to myself to try and find out. I must keep my word to John White, who risked his house and possessions to save us. Above all, I think of Elizabeth the Queen who, with unfailing perception, saw deep inside the heart of a young girl and offered both compassion and redemption.

Chapter 22

Horses On Board

WE STAY WITHIN our small confines for most of the trip, a terrible constraint on us all. The great ship rocks and moans in the rough winter sea, tossing from side to side. Most of the time, we're seasick. The only ones who seem unaffected are the babes. They laugh and play, eat when hungry and sleep whenever weariness overtakes them.

When the storms subside and the sea is relatively calm, I've begun exploring the depths of the ship. It gives me something to do. Akaiyan frowns upon this but accompanies me always, so I'll not run into trouble. The few seamen we meet give us a wide berth, for I'm as Indian as Akaiyan and obviously, their orders are to leave us alone. But I've heard sounds which lead me to believe there are horses on board. As always, I'm drawn to the large animals like ants to Mistress Steueens' sweet honey.

I hear them one night after tossing and turning. The sounds are so familiar. Above the splash of the waves and the groans of the vessel, I can hear low neighing and soft snorting. I start up from my pallet. Immediately, Akaiyan is awake beside me, his hand on my arm.

"What is it?"

"*A hots*," I whisper so as not to disturb the others. "I can hear *a hots*."

"Not on this ship," he replies softly. "You told me the English don't carry such animals on board."

"Indeed, up to now they haven't. But I distinctly heard them calling."

And so we slip out of the small cabin, heading to where I think I heard the sounds. We step over sleeping bodies and rough-whiskered men. As on the Red Lyon, these sailors sleep wherever they can find a place. No one is disturbed. We move cautiously, for Akaiyan has taught me well. We traverse the entire ship until we reach a large holding area. I was right. For tethered in the dark bowels of this merchant ship are several horses, at least six. They're all mares.

Akaiyan gasps to see them. For the English horses are larger than the Spanish *caballos*, longer in leg and body. But what beauties they are, dark chestnuts and bays and one of purest white. Akaiyan goes immediately to her. She skitters and pulls away at first, then relaxes under his gentle touch.

"I have never seen an *a hots ware-occa*, white," he whispers. "I did not know there were such creatures."

"She's a beauty," I say, stroking her soft nose. "I wonder why this ship's transporting them?"

Our questions remain unanswered throughout the entire voyage. I can only surmise that the English are learning from their enemy Spain. Horses in the New World have always given the Spanish conquistadors an edge.

"They should have a stallion," I tell Akaiyan, "in order

to enlarge their stock."

I think immediately of Diablo and Thunderer back on Croatoan Island. If we could but bring the white one with us, she'd make beautiful babes and enrich our herd with her English blood. But the thought is a wild one and I put it out of my mind.

Many a night, Akaiyan and I slip out and visit the a hots' quarters. They've become familiar with our smell and nicker softly in greeting when we come among them. The white one I've named Regal, after our most royal Elizabeth. It seems only fitting to give her a *nickreruroh* name. She is, indeed, beautiful in every way. Her legs are long and slender; her tail curves in an arc; her mane is flowing; her eyes deep and luminous. The white of her muzzle gives way to a soft speckled pink near her lips, which move gently over my hand. I try to bring her something every time I come, though there's little enough to share.

Then one night just before dawn when we're ready to go back to our quarters, an old sailor discovers us. He gasps in surprise when he sees us amidst the horses, petting and stroking them. I quickly put a finger to my lips.

"Please don't call, for we mean them no harm."

"You speak English?" he asks dumbfounded, no doubt, to hear his native tongue flow from an Indian's lips.

"We've been granted safe passage to the New World. I've been at court. It's Elizabeth's wish that we be returned without harm."

I'm sorry now that I've said anything. But the old seafarer is in awe of the fact that I've held audience with the Queen. He just nods his head, puts a finger to his own lips and backs away. I can smell the whiskey on his breath. Even if he should talk, the others will think it's the liquor. I fervently hope so.

Chapter 23

The Western Ocean

THE WESTERN OCEAN has become our pathway home. The large merchant ship plows steadily onward, the fierce winds catching at its sails, threatening to rip them to shreds. At such times, the sailors lower the canvas hastily, then spend much time repairing the rips torn by the wind. In spite of that, we cut our prow through the waters leaving England far behind. In my mind's eye, I can see Croatoan Island beckoning. It's a comforting thought.

Our routine is one of dullness. For we awaken, feed our babes, play with them, go topside when the captain allows, then return below for our evening meal. Then off to sleep once more. The only break comes when Akaiyan and I can slip out at night to visit with the beautiful mares.

We haven't seen the old seafarer since that one time. I'm certain that in his drunken stupor, he must have thought us apparitions. Most of the crewmen believe we're all Indians; they give us a wide berth. I've not had another occasion to use

English, speaking in Croatoan to the others, even Enrique. For not a word of the Spanish tongue should be uttered, lest the crew take it upon themselves to hurl him overboard in their anger which rages still against Spain and her ships. The crew believes we're being returned to our native land; the captain has our papers guaranteeing safe passage.

The English captain is a much older man than was Richard Fendler. He's broad of shoulder and sports a lusty beard. But his manner is kind with us. No doubt he was chosen by Master Burghley as one in whom the Queen could place her complete trust. I've no worries as to his lusting after our women, and the sailors under his command are reasonable with manners. At least, they don't curse around us, which is a comfort in itself. But when off duty, they consume the spirits and we do well to avoid crossing their paths.

There are two English gentlemen on board, one old, the other youngish, about twenty-five or so. They might be father and son, though I'm not privy to that information. They keep much to themselves and I've only seen them from a distance. They're well-dressed and carry themselves like proper gentlemen. On one occasion, I saw the younger one peering through his spyglass at our little group. The babes were playing in one corner of the deck during a rare time we were allowed above. Te-lah-tai, Ooteinne and Twah-ne were watching the children, while Akaiyan, Enrique and I enjoyed a moment of quiet. I suddenly felt unnerved.

Looking across the deck, I saw the young gentleman staring at me. In spite of the distance separating us, my face grew red with embarrassment. I lowered my head and turned my back toward him. A few moments later when I looked, he was gone.

I wonder what two English gentlemen are doing sailing

this merchant ship? Perhaps they're emissaries for Her Majesty, seeking to establish new trade routes. Perhaps they're doing what Master White must have done, as Ralph Lane, Thomas Hariot and Richard Hakluyt did before him, seeking new territories wherein to establish yet another colony. In either case, I know nothing of their intentions. But they intrigue me.

A fierce storm sweeps down from the north. Winds tear a sail to shreds; the great ship groans and protests. The waves sweep across her bow, threatening to swamp us. No wonder the pirates don't traverse these waters in winter. Their ships would be capsized. But this merchant vessel weathers it all. We lose one man to the storm; great waves wash across the deck and carry a sailor overboard. There's nothing to be done, for he's lost immediately in the raging sea. Enrique and I say Christian prayers for his soul so it might speed to Heaven. I wonder if Heaven's doors are open to such rough men, though Father always said that Our Dear Lord is merciful in His judgment. Enrique and I cross ourselves and say the "Our Father," while Akaiyan and the others watch.

Even I'm seasick as the ship plunges and rises in the waves. The bile bucket overflows and the stench is unbearable. The babes fret and cry for there's nothing for them to do. No one can keep any food down. The wind howls around the ship, tearing at its planking. Not even on The Red Lyon were there such storms as this one, for we sailed in spring and summer. This winter storm with its winds and hail beats the ship almost into submission. The rigging goes down several times; thick ice forms upon the surface of the decks. We stay below and pray most fervently.

Chapter 24

The English Gentleman

I THINK I'VE LIVED my whole life upon a ship. In truth, I've traveled more ships than most girls my age; Mary and Alice back in England have never been on one. I should be at home equally on land or sea, but I can't wait for this voyage to end. For across the sea waiting for me, for Akaiyan and Enrique and all of us, is an island of incredible beauty. I dream of its sandy dunes, the tall grasses blowing in the wind, the thick strand of trees which shield it from the mainland.

I dream of seeing my mother once more. How will she look, I wonder? For it's been almost two years since I last saw her, her face filled with worry, her eyes bright with tears. How has my brother fared, no longer Thomas but Cauhau-wean, the young warrior? Will Manteo still be the same and Sinopa, who rules the Croatoan? Will the *a hots* still be galloping the dunes with Carlos and Quayah on their backs? Did Carlos survive his swim back to the island that fateful day so long ago? Has the filly Star grown to carry a man on her back?

Always, so many questions, so few answers.

The captain tells us we've been blown off course by the last storm. The bad weather has kept us from regaining our original path. He shakes his head and mutters under his breath. Often we see ice floes to port, to starboard. The wind is chill and we keep the babes below. Oohahn-ne has a bad cold and cries most of the day. At night, she keeps me awake with her heavy breathing.

I've now seen the English gentlemen on several occasions. Once they walked right past where we're quartered and no doubt heard the children crying. Another time, I almost ran into the younger one while taking some fresh air topside. Enrique was with me, keeping his face covered as much as possible. For he doesn't look *unqua*, no matter how dark his skin, nor English, no matter how hard he tries. When we saw the Englishman coming, we spoke softly in Croatoan. He paused but a second before continuing on his way. There's no reason to think he suspects anything.

He's quite a handsome man, if I judge him by English standards. My idea of handsome is, of course, my dear Akaiyan, with his finely-chiseled features and his deep dark eyes. This Englishman is brown-haired and brown-eyed. He sports a moustache and short beard. The older man is, indeed, his father and, from what I've managed to overhear, they're seeking to establish a place for a new settlement. They're men of wealth, with monies to invest in land. They own shares in Sir Walter Ralegh's company, formed to continue his interests in the New World. If Sir Walter is out of favor with Elizabeth, his ideas are still courted by men with money and power. They represent a company of merchants to whom he sold his charter, with much gold at their disposal.

And then one day, the young English gentleman speaks

to me. I find it strange for surely he believes me to be Indian, not knowing the English tongue at all. My heart leaps in my throat.

"I know you speak English," he says. We're standing by the mizzenmast. Akaiyan and Enrique haven't yet appeared. The wind has died down and I've come to take in great breaths of fresh salty air.

I shake my head, but his keen eye stares directly at me and my face reddens. I was never good at lying.

"Kind sir," I say then. "I am, indeed, English. My friends are Indians. Akaiyan is my husband and the father of my children. We're returning to Croatoan Island, our home."

"I've heard that you travel under Elizabeth's auspices, with papers marked with her Great Seal. How did you manage that?"

"We were held at her court for over seven months. I birthed my son there. She wished to learn about our lives in the New World. She welcomed us."

He shakes his head, pulling on his beard.

"Remarkable," he says then. "Our good Queen has always looked kindly upon what she calls, 'the Noble Savage.' "

"Indeed, sir, she calls Manteo and all the *unqua*, noble."

"How came you to marry one?"

"My parents sailed from Portsmouth in 1587. We built a colony upon Roanoak Island. Hostiles threatened our safety and the colony split in half; some went to Chesapeake, some to Croatoan. It's there that I met my husband."

"We must talk more," he says hastily, and I see his father approaching. When he sees my anxiety, he puts a finger to his lips,

"Your little secret is safe with me." He turns and leaves. I don't see him for over a week.

Chapter 25

Lover Of Horses

THE ENGLISHMEN SPEAK at great length with our captain, discussing shipping routes, charts and maps of unexplored territories. This has been told to me by the younger gentleman, whose name is Robert Ashbury. He seems to have taken me into his confidence, telling me of their plans for a new and much larger colony further up the coast from Roanoak. I, in turn, have told him of our experiences upon that island that was my first home, how we fared, the loss of George Howe, the elder, John Tydway and little Agnes. Tears fill my eyes at those sad memories.

I've told him of the splitting of our colony into two factions, our home upon Croatoan, how I led Eleanor Dare and the others through the inland wilderness. I've not spoken at all about Enrique and our escape from the Spanish garrison at Chesapeake. He's intrigued by my fluency with the *unqua* language; he admires my deerskin clothing and asks how it's fashioned. He's told me he's unmarried, for duty calls him to travel with his father as representatives of their joint-stock company.

Whenever his father appears, our discussions cease. I suspect that he's somewhat in awe, even afraid, of his father's sharp tongue. Equally, whenever Akaiyan or Enrique come topside, I turn from him to greet them, pretending that he's there merely by chance. Akaiyan, like young George Howe used to do with him, turns surly in his presence.

The ship plows onward, weathering storm after storm. We're weary of our confinement, the endless swell of water, the lack of decent food. But I keep my heart light, for all this can be endured for just one glimpse of my beloved Croatoan Island. I try to visit the *a hots* as much as possible, bringing them such small treats as I can manage to procure.

"She's a beauty," Master Ashbury says of Regal. He pats her neck. "I paid dearly for her."

"You had to pay?"

"Indeed. Such a prize costs a great deal. She'll be an asset to our venture. We'll breed her to a fine stallion."

"But you carry no male horses with you."

"I hear the Spanish stock are strong and fit. We'll find a worthy mate and erelong, there'll be a foal which combines the best of both."

"I thought the English hated anything Spanish."

"In truth, the only good thing the Spaniards have are their sturdy horses. It was my idea," he adds covertly. "My father wasn't in favor of transporting animals across the Western Ocean."

I wonder what courage this young man must have shown, to dispute his father's wishes and insist on bringing the mares. But I'm thankful he did. For the lovely horses are my solace and comfort when Oohahn-ne frets too much, or Caun-

reha is teething and keeps me up at night. I'm glad then to turn them over to Twah-ne, endlessly patient, and slip down to visit these beauties.

"You have a way with horses," Master Ashbury says, watching me stroke and caress Regal. "It's as if you were one with them."

"We have *a hots* back on Croatoan Island," I tell him.

"Indeed, and how did your Indian friends manage to get horses?"

"Captured from Spanish soldiers," I smile. He smiles back.

"So we both know the value of some Spanish things, eh?"

He turns then and leaves abruptly, for my dear Akaiyan has appeared, and his eyes are darker than ever with the anger inside.

"I forbid you to speak with him," Akaiyan says.

"You can't forbid me," I retort. "I'll speak to whomever I wish."

"A good *kateocca* listens to her husband."

"Perhaps I'm not a good wife, then."

"I am your husband. You must obey me in all things."

I run from him and seek solace with Ooteinne. My eyes are wet with tears. It is, after all, our first real argument.

"It is not good for an *unqua* woman to be seen with any man other than her husband," Ooteinne explains.

"There was no harm, we were merely talking."

"Akaiyan is young and headstrong. Perhaps you would do well to have some time alone with him. I will see what I can do."

Though I don't know how she does it, Ooteinne manages to move our children and the others to another small place for the night, so Akaiyan and I can be alone. She brushes her lips against my cheek, an English custom she's acquired, and draws the canvas partition down.

At first, my husband is still angry and turns his back, sitting cross-legged on the planked floorboards. But when I go over and place my hands upon his shoulders, he turns suddenly and pulls me down with passion. We kiss and embrace and for a few hours, that small musty cabin with its hard wooden floor is a place where the angels sing.

I'm much more discreet after that, making sure that when the Englishmen are walking the deck, I'm below. I'm usually safe going at night to the *a hots'* quarters, for no one is about.

"Oh, beautiful Regal," I whisper one night as she blows warm breath against my skin. "Sweet Regal. How I wish you were mine. I'd ride you up and down the sandy dunes. You'd like Croatoan, I know it. Perhaps Diablo or Thunderer would be your mate. What a beautiful foal you'd make."

I wrap my arms about her curved neck. She whickers low in her throat. Unconsciously, my hands finger the amulets around my neck. One is from Akaiyan, given as my wedding present. It contains silver shells and special good-luck beads. The other holds the wooden horse that Manteo carved for me so long ago. I take it out carefully. Against the silver of the moon's light shining through a slim opening, the wood gleams like polished marble.

"Do you see, sweet Regal, the symbol carved by Manteo. To his people, all *a hots* are like gods of the wind, of the sun itself."

Something falls to the ground with a soft thud. It's the bracelet that Eleanor gave me for my birthday. Dangling from it is the golden lion with its diamond eyes. I'd almost forgotten about it, tucked so long inside the leather pouch. I quickly pick it up and slip it over my wrist. This is the bracelet Ananyas gave to her. She loved it so. But she loved me more, I think, and once again, tears fill my eyes. Where is she now? Is she safe and happy? Has she met up with George Howe and the others? Surely she deserves some happiness, for she's left behind a dead husband and child. I kneel and cross myself, to pray for the souls of those departed, and for the safety of our brave colonists, wherever they may be.

Chapter 26

The Attack

A SHIP IS SEEN off the starboard bow bearing down upon us. It's impossible to tell its flag through the mists but even so, the flag could be a false one, as pirates are wont to do. Though I'd thought none sailed the wintery seas, it's obvious this vessel is either pirate or Spanish. The alarm has been sounded, the cannons readied, the men with arms await the captain's word.

We huddle together in our small, cramped quarters, keeping the babes amused, trying not to scare them. How could we ever survive a battle? What if we should sink? No one could last long in these freezing waters. I say many prayers, both Christian and *unqua*, for our safety.

A cannon shot booms in our ears, but lands far short of us. Is it an attack or a signal that they're heaving to, close to our starboard side? I learn later that the captain hails them, asking what flag they fly under. The fearsome pirate's flag is hoisted swiftly. A second cannon shot lands nearer its mark, the waters splashing up over some of our sailors. The captain responds with cannon fire of his own. The battle is joined.

The pirate ship is of much smaller size. To even dream of attacking our large merchant vessel shows a foolhardy leader. But they must be desperate for supplies. The captain tells us later they were blown off course by the same winter storm that changed our path. Their small ship was almost capsized by the waves, nearly plunging them to a watery grave. The men threatened mutiny, insisting their captain find a stouter vessel they could plunder and board. At the risk of his own neck he ordered the firing of his cannons against us, though he knew it was a losing battle from the start.

Our cannons belch fire and smoke; round after round is shot. The sails of the pirate ship are ripped to shreds; their masts crack and fall. Great holes appear in their hull, through which the freezing water pours in. Their bow points skyward as they slip beneath the waves. All are lost, it seems.

But no, several men are pulled aboard, shivering and chilled to the bone. They're quickly taken below, their fate unknown to us. All I care about is our safety and that of the *a hots*. Were any hurt? Has anyone been down to see them, to calm them?

We've sustained very little damage. The great ship has lost a sail; a portion of the deck railing has been blown away. But there's no permanent damage to our hull. The men can mend the sail and fix the railing. Our captain seems quite cheerful. He comes down to tell us the news himself, bringing with him the cook who gives us extra food and some soup he managed to keep in the pot. It's hot and nourishing. Our babes take it eagerly and so do we, for the winter chill seeps into our bones and we ache with cold.

As soon as possible, I leave my babes with Twah-ne, giving her a quick kiss on the cheek, and slip with Akaiyan down to the animals' shelter. But I needn't have worried. Young Master Ashbury is down there already, soothing the fretful mares, whispering in their ears, stroking their necks. Akaiyan mutters when he sees him and tries to pull me away. But I won't leave. So Akaiyan waits with me. He can't be angry for long, however, not with the *a hots* near. He goes to one and begins whispering soft words to her. She nuzzles his shoulder.

"Such beauties," says Master Robert, "they were so frightened. Cannons should be outlawed."

"The cannons saved our lives and this ship," I reply, petting Regal. I see she has a small wound upon her haunch. The blood trickles slowly down.

"What happened?"

"She panicked and caught herself against the planking. But it's nothing, I assure you."

I gently wipe the blood away, petting her all the while. She trembles under my touch, then calms down. Akaiyan comes over to see. The wound is clean and shouldn't fester. I slip her a piece of sugar, a rare treat I've managed to procure.

"Come," says Akaiyan, once again pulling on my arm.

"You go," I tell him. "I want to stay with Regal."

He goes and I'm alone, for Master Robert has also left.

"Sweet Regal," I whisper. "Don't worry, your wound isn't deep. Soon you'll be better."

Then I sense someone's presence behind me. It's Master Robert, who's returned when he saw Akaiyan leaving. He stands there for a few moments watching me.

"A magnificent animal," he says at last. I nod my head.

"Quite beautiful," he continues. I hear him cough. "And you, also," he says then, turning me abruptly around. Before I can say a word, he kisses me. Then he backs away, his face as red as mine.

"I shouldn't have... I had no right...."

"Indeed, sir, I'm a married woman...."

"But quite lovely," he whispers. "Quite lovely...."

He turns and leaves, silent as a shadow while I stand trembling by Regal's side, my thoughts a jumble, my heart beating fast.

Chapter 27

Choices

IT'S A STRANGE feeling, indeed, to be desired by two men. One is my husband, my chosen love. He's an Indian, an *un-qua*, whose people are now my people. The other is a stranger to me, yet of my blood and background. Our ancestors sprang from the same soil; we revere our English Queen and bow to English law. With Akaiyan, there is no such link. Only my passion for him, my love, my giving of myself and the bearing of his children. How can I dismiss all that?

My heart is racing as I return to Akaiyan and the others. Surely my face will reveal what's just happened. But they're sleeping when I enter our small quarters. Akaiyan stirs and mumbles something as I settle next to him. I reach over and touch his cheek lightly with my fingers. He kisses my hand and settles back into sleep. I'm awake all night.

I don't see Master Robert for several days, but my face reddens whenever I think of his lips on mine. Though I didn't kiss him back, nor passion surge within me, it was still an illicit kiss; Mother would frown on such happenings and chide me severely, saying I was wrong to be alone with the *a hots*. So for these few days, I don't go down to visit gentle Regal and the others without Akaiyan by my side, my faithful shadow.

Oohahn-ne's cold is gone, for which I give great thanks. We've no proper physician on board who can minister to a sick child. She's become her merry self again, playing with Caun-reha and laughing as she sings with Te-lah-tai and the others. What a sweet little girl she is. I sometimes like to sit and watch her, fascinated as she discovers each new and wondrous thing. I can remember little Virginia doing the same thing; how marvelous to view life through a child's eyes.

Master Robert keeps to the far end of the ship talking earnestly with his father or the captain, poring over maps and charts. Occasionally, when he doesn't notice, I watch him from my safe haven, playing with Oohahn-ne and glancing up every now and then. I'm not drawn to him as I was to Akaiyan, yet he's the first man other than my husband to kiss me. The touch is different, the shape of the lips, the tickling of the moustache. He smelled slightly of tobacco and mint; his mouth tasted of sweet wine. Perhaps he'd sipped a glass of sherry to bolster his courage; perhaps he'd planned it so, to be down there when I came.

How might he have felt seeing me walk in with Akaiyan? And what relief to see my husband leave, then to slip back inside where he could find me alone? Are men really capable of such subterfuge? It's said that women, not men, are the ones who plan and scheme to meet young men and lay their traps, like spiders spinning webs.

"Come into my parlor," says the spider to the fly, and in walks the young man totally unaware. The woman, dressed in her fanciest silk and lace, flutters her eyelashes and looks demure. Her face reddens, her lip trembles; the young man thinks she might swoon. Before she can faint, he lightly kisses her hand. The trap is sprung!

Alice and Mary, and all the young girls of my youth, were thus taught; how to entice and catch an eligible man. And until we sailed the rough seas to another land and I learned the ways of the gentle *unqua*, I, too, thought much the same way.

Our lives continue on. Master Robert avoids me like the plague; I content myself with playing with my two children, helping Te-lah-tai and Ooteinne with their babes. Twah-ne is as an older sister might be, patient and loving, relieving us whenever we're tired.

I miss Regal too much to stay away for long. She reminds me of the horses back on Croatoan: Beauty, Star, Chaunoctay, Hoonoch, Utchar and the others. I often think I must have been an *a hots* in a previous lifetime, then laugh at such a ridiculous notion. More and more, Akaiyan grows sullen. *Unqua* can't be confined; they need to be free like the wind and the stars. Too much in John White's house; too much in these small, cramped quarters. I'm sometimes glad to leave, not to see his mouth turned down, hear his words terse and sharp.

Regal snorts into my hand, her whiskered lips tickling my palm. She's nibbled all the oats I've given her. There's nothing left. I stroke her sleek neck, wrapping my fingers into her mane.

"Beautiful Regal, sweet girl. I'd love to see you race the dunes and splash in the water's edge."

"You're drawn to her like a magnet," says Master Robert Ashbury, stepping from the shadows. His cloak is off his shoulders, his shirt open at the collar. His face is red and he lowers his eyes.

"Forgive me for intruding," he continues, "but I, like

you, am fascinated by the horses, this one in particular."

"I wish she were mine," I comment then for want of anything else to say.

"And what would you do with her?"

"Mate her to one of our stallions. Her breeding would enrich our herd."

"Would you ride her?"

"Like the wind."

"Dear Jess," he says then, coming forward and taking my hand. "I'd give her to you as a present... if only... if only...."

"If only what?"

"You'd leave your Indian and come with me."

When I say nothing, boldness takes hold of him.

"I can offer you everything, anything your heart desires. Why should you dress like a Savage? What future lies ahead for you, the squaw of an Indian? Let me take you away from all this... this starkness, this unhappy life. Only say the word...."

I stand there as he kisses my fingers and places my hand against his cheek.

"Dear Jess, say you'll come with me. I wish to marry you...."

Chapter 28

"1 Am An Unqua"

SEAGULLS ARE SIGHTED circling in the grey sky. They wheel and dip crying their loud mewing cries. They signal our approach to land, a coastline still far off in the distance. How glad I am to see them flying!

"Look at the birds, look at the *oosnooqua*, feather," I say to Oohahn-ne and Caun-reha, for one has drifted down to lie upon the rough deck. I pick it up and stroke it longingly. Then I tickle both children under their chins, upon their cheeks. They giggle and laugh.

There's a light-hearted feeling now among us all. The endless winter sea with its ice floes, its storms, will soon be a part of memory only. I sniff the wind hoping to smell the land, but there's nothing.

Akaiyan has come on deck with me. Now he slips his hand about my waist protectively and leans down to kiss my neck. His ways are warm and familiar; his habits more English than he'd care to admit. Certainly, our customs have

rubbed off on him.

"I will be glad to be home," he says gently in Croatoan. "I wish to see my father, my *caunotka*. I left with one *woc-canookne* and return with two. Soon we will be together again in our own *oinouse*."

I say nothing. The words of Master Robert Ashbury have echoed in my ears for days: 'Dear Jess, say you'll come with me. I wish to marry you.' I've thought of nothing else, though I've tried not to. In my worst moments of despair, I've never felt so uneasy, so confused. If only Eleanor were here by my side, I could talk to her. If only Mother were nearby, I could get comfort from her wisdom. I've spent so many sleepless nights tossing and turning, sometimes coming up on deck to lean against the railing, watching the rolling waves. The great ship goes up and down leaving its mark upon the waters, the white splash of foam from its bow, the curving wake trailing behind. Each roll of the wave brings me closer to those I love, to the island which has been my home. Though the nights are cold and I shiver constantly, I stay above, trying to sort out the jumble of my thoughts.

Even if I no longer loved Akaiyan, how could I return to English life? It was so stiff and uncomfortable quartered in the palace. I felt so out of place dressed in homespun cotton to hold audience with the Queen. I can't picture myself in silk and lace, sitting at idle talk with ladies of society, engaging in conversation, or listening to my husband and his friends discussing politics. And how would my babes be received? What hushed whispers would be heard, what muffled laughter behind my back at the little 'half-breed' children?

What would Mother say? Take what you know and make count of all the good. Does it outweigh the bad? What would Eleanor say? Follow your heart, for life takes too quickly those we love.

Indeed, I love Akaiyan. Of that, there's no doubt! I listen sometimes to his rhythmic breathing when we're sleeping, his arm flung across me, his warm body pressed against mine. I think of his loving me, his fire and passion, his look upon holding Oohahn-ne or Caun-reha. I remember him sitting astride Diablo, clinging to the stallion's mane, his body one with him as they gallop across the dunes. I'm glad to be his *kateocca*.

And then one dark night, I imagine I can smell the land we're approaching. I breathe in the sweet fragrance of earth, though still veiled in darkness and many miles away. I close my eyes while leaning against the railing and hear the thunder of hooves upon the ground, the songs of women at the hearth, the laughter of children playing. I hear, not the heavy groan of a ship, but the echo of wind in the leaves, the sigh of dune grasses pressed almost to the sand, the splashing of waves against a familiar shore. My heart turns toward home, my face turns away from England. I hear Elizabeth speaking clearly,

"Go back to your happiness, your Noble Savages. You are the lucky one, if you had but the good sense to see."

"Master Ashbury," I say to him the very next day. "Wherein lies your destination?"

"The Virginia coast," he answers, turning from the *a hots* to see me standing there. "It's a pleasure to see you here once more. I've missed you."

"Master Ashbury...," I start to say.

"Please call me Robert."

I pick up a brush and begin to groom Regal. The gash on her haunch has healed nicely. I gently trace the thin scar.

"Master Ashbury, I wish you well in your endeavors. I

know that you and your father will find riches waiting. The lands of Virginia are just beckoning for new colonists, new settlements."

"Dear Jess," he says then, coming toward me. "What say you of my proposal? Will you come with me?"

I hold my head up and look at him fairly, the handsome face of a handsome young English gentleman filled with hope and expectation.

"Master Ashbury," I say, my words calm and quiet, suddenly at peace with myself. "I'm called Little Bird, and I am an *unqua*."

Chapter 29

Hataraske Landing

WE WEIGH ANCHOR at Hataraske three days later and for yet a fourth day we stay on board, for the sea is too rough even in the sheltered inlet for small boats to breach the waves.

Such excitement fills the air. We've gathered our meager belongings and are ready to board the small crafts which will carry us to land. From Hataraske, we'll journey to Croatoan Island. Akaiyan's face is full of joy.

Master Robert Ashbury the younger has avoided me altogether, staying close to his father and the captain. His face reddens whenever he glances my way. Having made my decision, my heart is light and I turn eagerly to thoughts of my dearest mother, my beloved *a hots*. My only sorrow is to leave beautiful Regal, for I've grown attached to her beyond belief.

"Sweet Regal," I say, leaning my head against her smooth satiny neck. "I must leave you now to go home, while you journey on up the coast. I can't bear to say goodbye."

Tears trickle down my cheeks. Regal nuzzles me with

her velvet nose. I scratch behind her ears. Saying goodbye has never been easy for me, always accompanied by tears and a heavy heart.

Akaiyan has come with me and he, too, is saddened at the thought of leaving the lovely mare. He whispers *unqua* words to her. She paws the ground and blows through her nostrils.

"But think," says Akaiyan when he sees my tears, "of the *a hots* who will welcome you home. The two stallions, my *utte-wiraratse* who must now be fully grown. You will love to ride her like the wind."

I close my eyes, imagining little Star as a full-grown mare able to carry me upon her broad back. What pleasure it will be to ride her across the fields and into the sandy dunes. A faint smile traces my lips.

"We've been gone so long," I whisper, then giving Regal one last kiss, turn and run from the *a hots'* quarters. To stay longer will only cause more pain.

The next morning the sun shines brightly. Though the wind is cold, the sea has calmed somewhat. The boats are lowered with us in them. I wave goodbye to the captain, giving thanks for our safe journey and our arrival here at Hataraske. Moments after our boats touch the waves, a loud yelling is heard above us.

"Wait," calls Master Ashbury, "I'm coming. I'll see you safely to shore."

Akaiyan frowns, hunching his shoulders and turning his face away. I frown also, for this may serve only to complicate matters. But to my great surprise, a large flat raft is lowered from the great vessel and tethered on board, the white mare. She's covered with a blanket against the wind and her eyes are blindfolded. Master Ashbury holds her bridle tightly, whilst the flat raft rocks precariously as it settles in the water. Five men accompany him and they steer and row the cumbersome raft after our small boats.

We land but a few moments later, our boats scraping the sandy bottom. Akaiyan, Enrique and the others jump out, dragging the boats to high ground. We stand on native soil for the first time in months. The ground rushes up to meet us and Te-lah-tai and the others almost fall. I remember my father's words, "Our legs have grown accustomed to the roll of the ship. It will take a while to feel steady."

I tell Akaiyan to go ahead, leading the way for the others. I've given my babes into the care of Twah-ne and Ooteinne. Now I wait to see Master Ashbury for one last time. My husband doesn't want to leave, but I insist. He trudges up the beach, his face sullen, his eyes once again bright with anger. I watch the cumbersome raft rock in the shallows, to see Master Ashbury lead Regal down into the waters. She tries to rear, but he quiets her and runs her up the sand near to where I'm standing.

"What game is this?" I ask, for he's taken the blindfold off and the blanket covering her. She sees me and thrusts her long neck forward.

"No game," he replies. "A gift, my gift to you."

I stare like a fool. Only when he hands the reins over to me, do I come awake.

"I can't accept such a gift," I say then, handing the reins back. He shakes his head.

"Try to be gracious," he says with a sad wry smile. "I thought to myself, she won't have me, she won't leave her husband. This I must admire. But I want to give her something. What can I give to a woman who obviously has all she needs and wants? Then I remembered your love for Regal. She's yours. In truth, she belongs to you for she's given her heart. See how she... loves you."

The white mare is nuzzling my neck, my shoulder. My hair is intertwined with her silver mane. Tears are flowing down my face.

"But your father...."

"Regal is mine," he states emphatically. "to keep or to give away. Take her.... remember me...."

He turns quickly and runs back into the shallows, climbing aboard the raft. The men push it and the other boats away from shore. He waves but once, then turns his face toward the great merchant ship waiting. His destiny lies up the coast. I say a silent prayer to wish him God-speed. Then I lead Regal to where the others stand quietly waiting.

Chapter 30

Croatoan Island

AND WE ARRIVE once more on the shores of Croatoan. I kneel down and say a prayer, holding the reins of the beautiful white mare. Regal snorts and lowers her head, nibbling at my hair. Oohahn-ne and Caun-reha squirm to get down from Twah-ne and Akaiyan who've been carrying them. They race up and down on the sand. I laugh watching them.

For most of the short journey north I've ridden Regal, feeling the way she moves, the effortless of her gait, the smoothness of her rhythm. At one point, I let her have free rein and she gallops away from my small group, my body one with hers, my hands entangled in her mane. She slows when I call her name, responding to my voice with no fretting. She wheels in the sand and turns back at the pressure of my knees. Akaiyan watches us with his mouth open. For even Diablo and Thunderer can't move as she.

"She's the wind," I call to Akaiyan, "she's sunlight and stars and moon. She's heaven to ride!"

He takes a turn then, marveling at her quickness and ease of gait. She handles without effort; there's none of the heaviness of the Spanish *caballos*. Her long legs and lighter bones make her appear weightless. Akaiyan is enchanted.

"Wait until my father sees her," he says joyously. "He will not believe in such an *a hots*."

It's March on Croatoan Island. The first buds are appearing on the trees. Spring is coming; our lives are reborn once more. Mother runs from her house at the news of our arrival. She's weeping and laughing at the same time. She doesn't know who to hug first, me or Akaiyan or my children. Her mouth drops open when she sees Oohahn-ne and Caun-reha.

"He looks like your father," she gasps, then drops to her knees in prayer.

"His name is William Arnold," I tell her, my hands upon her shoulders. "But I call him Caun-reha. It means little panther."

Mother's hair is streaked with much gray. Her face is creased and lined. But when I see her smile, she hasn't aged at all, so young and beautiful she seems to me. My brother, Thomas, now known as Cauhau-wean, is a man, an *unqua quottis*. He's taller than I, almost as tall as Akaiyan. He leans down to kiss my cheek, his eyes full of tears. Then he swings Oohahn-ne high in the air. She giggles hysterically.

Manteo greets us stoically, his hands stretched out toward his son. His hair, too, is streaked gray and his shoulders seem more bent. He walks with a limp.

"Last winter," Quayah tell us, "an *oochehara* raided our goats. He left his mark on my father, but my father wears his claws and teeth."

Indeed, the long scar runs down the length of Manteo's leg. Around his neck is the necklace of bear claws and teeth, a sign of his triumph.

"It is good to see my son and his *kateocca* again," Manteo says. "And *necte woccanookne*, two children. My son's seed is strong."

I fairly blush and lower my head. For deep in my womb, another child grows, Akaiyan's child. I will become a mother again in late November.

"Your children are beautiful," cries Mother. She hasn't stopped crying since we first appeared. She hugs Oohahn-ne, then Caun-reha, then Oohahn-ne again.

Quayah has grown taller also. He gleams with pride at the sight of his older brother. He gasps, like the others, at the white mare.

"She is a ghost," he whispers. The *unqua* women put their hands over their faces.

"No," I laugh. "She's a horse of the English, a thorough-bred. Her blood will mingle with our *a hots'*, and we'll have many fine foals."

Quayah reaches a hand out to touch Regal. She blows warm breath into his palm. He gently strokes her.

And then I see Carlos. I hug him tightly.

"I thought you were lost in the sea," I sob, remembering how he threw himself over the side of the boat that day long ago. "I thought you'd been drowned."

He shakes his head.

"The sea spat me up on the beach," he smiled. "And I've taken care of *los caballos* for you and Enrique."

We walk to the *a hots'* shelter. Familiar neighs greet me as I enter. There's Beauty and Chaunoctay, as gentle as ever. Diablo stamps a hoof and then lowers his head.

"He remembers how I used to scratch his ears," I laugh, doing just that. "And where's Star?"

"Over here," says Carlos, pointing to a beautiful bay mare with a white, five-pointed star on her forehead. I gasp. For Star is all grown up. Will she remember me?

Star butts me with her head. She nuzzles my neck.

"You do remember," I whisper. "Little Star, I love you so."

"Qui-heiratse has a new foal also," says Carlos. "Another girl. We've named her Koo-awatse. Isn't she beautiful?"

The little *hembra* is almost a year old. She hides behind her chestnut dam and peeks out. Soon she'll get to know me, to know us all.

"Where's Thunderer and Utchar, Fawn and the foals, Hoonoch and Cotcoo-rea?"

"At Enrique's lodge," says Carlos, "where I've been staying. Hoonoch and Cotcoo-rea are grown now."

I give a great sigh. For it's been so long, of course they've all grown. I'll see them soon, I'll see them all just as soon as I can.

Chapter 31

English Memories

"HOW DID YOU manage an audience with Her Majesty?"

I blush.

"I'm afraid I made a nuisance of myself, bothering Master White so much that he'd no choice but to arrange it."

Mother and I are with Mistress Steueens and Wenefrid Powell. My two children and Wenefrid's play together in a corner. Since we last were together, Wenefrid has had another child, a girl whom she calls Regine. We watch the children for a while, then resume our discussion.

"What's she like?" Wenefrid leans closer, as does Mistress Steueens.

"Very regal," I try to remember. How can I tell them about Elizabeth? Their memories are of stories they've heard, perhaps a glimpse of a carriage passing through the streets. How can I tell them of how she was with me, watching me give birth in her private chambers, following her as she swept up the Tower steps to see Enrique?

How can I explain the womanly part of her, her sigh when she spoke of the intrigue at her court, the longing I saw deep within for a child of her own? They know only the Elizabeth who sits upon the throne, who ordered the execution of her cousin, Mary Queen of Scots, who levied taxes, who laid to waste the Spanish Armada within the channel waters. Mother sees my face and takes my hand.

"Perhaps my Jess has seen the real woman behind the throne."

I squeeze Mother's hand gently and nod my head. She understands, of course, without my saying another word. We sit together in silence, save only for the laughter of the children playing behind us.

"She's a good person," Mother says later when we're alone, "to provide you safe passage and to free Enrique."

"There were times of great despair, Mother," I reply, "when I didn't know what my fate, our fate, would be."

Then Mother asks her burning question.

"Do you wish you were still in London, and not on this island?"

I shake my head.

"I made my choice and it's here with you, with all the *un-qua*."

She sighs but goes about her cooking. I wonder if my dear mother would have made a similar choice, given the same opportunity to stay in London? She knows nothing of Master Robert Ashbury and his proposal. Why haven't I yet told her? I can't explain it, except that she might chide me for being foolish and not accepting his offer of marriage. But when I see her laughing with Oohahn-ne and my son, when I've revealed the news of my third child, there's no question in my mind that I made the right decision.

Upon seeing Twah-ne and Ooteinne, there's much fussing on the part of their husbands. Ooteinne holds her head high and proffers her girl child, Auhoorah, to her husband. He shakes his head and turns away. She weeps copious tears but he's adamant. Even though Manteo takes him aside and speaks with him, he still refuses to have anything to do with her. He plans to divorce her and there's nothing we can do.

Twah-ne's husband is an older man, almost as old as Manteo in years. He shakes his head when he hears their story then, just as we think he might turn away, extends his hand to Twah-ne. She goes to him joyfully and they enter their lodge house together. Ooteinne's cheeks are wet with tears, even while she kisses Auhoorah. Mother embraces her and leads her quietly into her lodge house. She will live with my dear mother and raise her child alone.

But *unqua* children are never alone. They belong to the village, to all the people. Ooteinne will live in Mother's lodge house; Auhoorah will be the child of all Chacandepeco, this village home. I kiss little Caun-reha on his fat cheeks; I give Oohahn-ne an extra hug.

The divorce ceremony is incredibly simple. It's dignified, belying the sorrow hidden beneath. Ooteinne's husband goes before Sinopa who takes a piece of buckskin, first winding it about his wrist and then, cutting it with her *oosocke nauh*. The severed pieces fall to the ground. Sinopa's face is lined with sadness, for it's almost unheard of for a man to divorce his wife. But her husband can't bear the thought of another man's touch upon her; nor another man's child in her arms. He goes into the woodlands for several days and nights, communing with the spirits. Ooteinne weeps, then rises from her bed of sorrows to take part once more in village life. The other women don't ostracize her, for her rape and pregnancy

were not of her choosing. Little Auhoorah wanders from hearth to hearth, being fed and played with. Several of the women come to visit Ooteinne at my mother's lodge house. Ooteinne's husband may or may not marry again. As for Ooteinne, there's one who smiles upon her as she passes through the village. Soon, I think, Karchai may ask for her hand in marriage. He's much older and not so handsome, but he will make her a good husband and be a father to Auhoorah.

Chapter 32

Beautiful Regal

MOTHER'S TIME IS now occupied with Ooteinne and her little one, as well as my two boisterous children. Oohahn-ne is into everything, exploring, examining. Caun-reha follows her example.

"I declare," exclaims my dear mother, "I've not the patience I once had."

Ooteinne has told me that she calls them Suzanne and William when I'm not around. At first I was annoyed but changed my mind. I want my children to know their English heritage as much as their *unqua* traditions. Mother lets Suzanne play with her silver spoons, a treasure she's carried with her from England. Master Powell has built a wooden doll house with intricate furniture, delighting my little girl. She plays for hours. William, on the other hand, bangs pots and pans loudly, stringing sentences together and chanting the nursery rhymes Mother and Mistress Steueens sing. Auhoorah joins in the singing. Mother has told Ooteinne that her name sounds much like Aurora, the dawn, so we now all call her Aurora.

While my children are so occupied and delighted, I spend as much time as I can with the *a hots*. Now that I've returned, they occupy a good part of my day. Enrique, Carlos and Quayah are fascinated with Regal. Never has a horse had so much attention! She dotes on it, nuzzling them and pushing her velvet nose into their hands at any occasion. I play with Star and Hoonoch and Cotcoo-rea; they're almost fully grown. I've ridden Star and the other two across the sandy dunes, as long I'd dreamed. When I'm on their backs, I feel like one with them.

But it's to Regal that I gravitate; her magic draws me always to her stall, a treat in my hands to entice her. And it's upon her back that I feel closest to God. The *unqua* feel the same closeness, I know. It's as if *a hots* were always a part of their lives. More and more, the village of Chacandepeco drift toward the animals as a source of their strength, the heart of their lives.

My child grows within me and soon Regal comes into her season. She frets and neighs low in her throat. She rubs her hind quarters against the wooden stall. There are no splinters in the wood to catch her haunches, Enrique has seen to that. She paws the ground and throws back her head. Her tail swings to one side in anticipation. Both Diablo and Thunderer sense she's in estrus and loud neighs ring through the village.

It's Enrique who decides to let Thunderer be the sire. He leads the large bay stallion into his compound, then returns for Regal. We all gather to watch, in awe of his aggressive nature as he mounts her. The young girls giggle and point, until Manteo frowns at them. There's a great deal of whinnying and thrashing, loud cries from both mare and stallion. Diablo's cries pierce the air also, so Quayah is sent to offer comfort for his loss. "Give him this," Carlos hands Quayah a carrot.

"It won't satisfy him," says Quayah. "Only the white mare will do that."

The two boys' mouths split into wide grins. When at last Thunderer has pleasured her, Enrique leads her back to her stall. The girls hover near Thunderer's fenced compound, talking in hushed whispers. I go to Regal and stroke her gently. "Well, my beautiful girl, did that please you? Will you now be quiet and content?"

A rush of warmth floods my whole being, for to watch the two *a hots'* courtship and mating stirs the memories of my own dear Akaiyan. I feel his hands slipping around my waist, his warm breath as he kisses my neck.

"I feel like a stallion," he whispers. "Come with me."

The child within kicks and moves slightly. I take Akaiyan's hand and place it upon my belly. He feels the movement and grins.

"You have given me my heart's delight," he says, kissing me gently. "I shall be the father of many."

I remember then my words to my mother upon the death of Eleanor's unborn child: "Mother, I'll have many children. I want lots."

She frowned and wept a little at my words. Now she plays with my daughter and son, and has hugged me tightly upon news of my third child. I'm thrilled to have this new babe for children are our link with the future, our ties to all that has come before and is yet to come.

Our village grows, and our herd of *a hots* as well. We are one in our strength!

Chapter 33

Christenings and A Wedding

THE WHOLE VILLAGE plans for the christenings of Caun-reha, Auhoorah and Rus-quauene, otherwise known as William, Aurora and Miguel. This is the name Enrique chose for his son. Te-lah-tai wrinkles up her nose when he announces it one evening, but he insists.

"*Miguel es el nombre de mi padre,*" he says emphatically. "He died when I was young. It's an honor to name my son after him."

Wenefrid Powell asks if little Regine can be included, for hers wasn't a proper ceremony at the time, so deep in mourning were they all during our absence. And the two *un-qua* women whose babes were born while we were away, have asked shyly if they can be a part of the celebrations. Ousrahti and Soo-Kahche smile and dress their babes in the finest *oc-ques* for the occasion.

Roger Bayley was killed by the pirates that long ago, fateful day, so Master Steueens steps up with his Bible in hand to read the blessed prayers. Master Steueens is a large, burly man. He strikes an imposing figure, the late afternoon sunlight framing his face.

"Bless these children, Lord Jesus," he says, sprinkling Holy Water on all six babes. Little Regine laughs, but the others cry, including my dear Caun-reha.

"Praise His Holy Name, and let the hearts of them that seek the Lord rejoice. Seek the Lord and His strength: Seek His presence always."

"*Ne unche, ne wartsauh, e youch se, tichke oonquera ee hitchra waure koone-hah,*" says Sinopa, "not one, not ten, but a hundred blessings upon all in the eyes of our Great Spirit."

We all cheer loudly. Then Master Steueens says each child's name, first in English, then in Croatoan. Again we cheer.

Then my own brother, Thomas, steps up to the front. Holding his hand is a young maiden, quite fair of face, called Sitchae. She's about sixteen. Mother's crying again.

"I am announcing to all the *unqua* and the *nickreruroh* that I plan to wed Sitchae."

She turns red, lowering her head. The village gives a mighty cheer. Mistress Steueens calls out,

"Hip, hip, hooray!"

"And I'm Cauhau-wean," he shouts, holding his other hand high in the air. "I ask Master Steueens to baptize me also."

Mother gasps and weeps some more, then finally nods her head. I run to put my arm about her shoulders.

"Be happy," I whisper. "Aren't you proud of your son?"

But she can't speak, for she's overcome with tears. Mistress Steueens takes her hand.

"A son is still a son, Sister Joyce, no matter what his

name. You're truly blessed, for soon you'll have so many grandchildren, you won't know what to do with them."

Mother begins to laugh, wiping furiously at her eyes. And so, the next week we see my brother Cauhau-wean married to Sitchae.

Sitchae's mother is dead so her father gives her away. She wears a tunic of white buckskin, bleached of its natural color. The beads and shells which adorn it have been sewn by many loving hands. She smiles shyly as she stands next to my beloved brother. Master Steueens again reads the ceremonial words. This time, Manteo officiates for the *unqua*.

"*Oonaquera, cotuch eets hitchra waure ki-yu-se*, a thousand times may the Great Spirit give you peace."

"And *muchos hijos*," smiles Enrique, while Te-lah-tai holds little Miguel.

"*Tewots utserosta*," says Te-lah-tai's mother, Ro-yaareh, "many children."

The riotous celebration lasts well into the evening. Mother gets drunk on fermented beer and lets herself be led back to her lodge house by Ooteinne. Cauhau-wean and Sitchae leave for their own lodge house. Akaiyan and I, Enrique and Te-lah-tai watch the sun set and sip the potent brew.

"Just a little," cautions Akaiyan. He's so solicitous, just like my dear father used to be. I lean my head against his shoulder. How strange, how wonderful, to see my young brother married. I no longer think of him as Thomas, but call him by his new name. I remember how excited he was when we first crossed the mighty ocean. He was only eleven and I, fourteen. He couldn't wait to explore this new land, nor wait to dress like the *unqua* and learn how to hunt and pull a bowstring.

Now he is truly an *entequos* with his very own *kateocca*. I give a great sigh.

"What's the matter?" Enrique asks.

"I've missed so much, my brother growing up. I remember him as a child and now he's a man, with a wife of his own. It's hard to believe."

"We all grow," says Enrique, stroking Te-lah-tai's hair. "Our son is almost six months old. I find that hard to believe."

The celebrations last well into the night. But Akaiyan and I have crept away to our lodge house, leaving the noise and laughter behind. I glance through the darkening shadows at my brother's new lodge house, and pray that he feels the joy that Akaiyan and I felt the night we were wed and, wondrously, still feel.

Chapter 34

The Oochehara Story

ALL THE LITTLE children struggle over their sounds and letters. I've begun teaching again, taking out Eleanor's slates and markers which she gave to me so long ago. Sinopa has asked the men to build a special lodge just for learning. She comes often to sit and watch me, smoking her long *oosquaana*. She's careful, though, to blow the smoke away from the children.

"You are a... good teacher," she searches for the English words. I nod my head in thanks. At first, I thought it would unnerve me to have Sinopa sitting within my classroom. But she often joins in, singing the songs I teach, clapping her hands in glee when a child gets a right answer.

"There are many different kinds of lessons," she continues, slipping into Croatoan. "Some are learned in the world of nature; others must be taught by the mother. And some need the skill of an *utquernare*, a teacher."

Very often, Sinopa herself becomes the teacher, shyly

sitting cross-legged in front of the children and telling them stories. I remember her story about the *che-ra* and why he feigns death when other animals are near. Today she tells about Manteo and his victory over the *oochehara*, bear.

"When Manteo was a *quottis*, his father sent him on his manhood training. He traveled many miles north across the waters. There were no *a hots* then to carry him."

She pauses to let that fact sink in. The children stare wide-eyed.

"He climbed many trees to look for the big *oochehara*. It was the season of the Traveling Moon, the leaves were turning red and gold, the air was chill. This was when the *oochehara* stuffed their bellies for the last time before their great winter sleep."

Sinopa places her cheek to rest upon her two joined hands. The children are fascinated for they've never heard this story before.

"While he was up a tree sitting on a branch, a big *oochehara* came shuffling up. On the branch where Manteo rested were large clusters of berries. The *oochehara* saw the berries and wanted them. She reached up and her long claws almost touched Manteo's leg. Manteo was like a statue, very quiet and still. Then the *oocherhara* smelled him. She roared a terrible roar, opening her mouth wide. Manteo's whole body could fit inside that mouth."

Again, she pauses for effect. No wonder Sinopa is called the Queen of Storytellers. I try not to smile.

"Quickly, Manteo tore off the cluster of berries and threw them into the *oochehara*'s mouth. Then he jumped off the branch and landed on her head. He spread his two feet on either side of her bony jaw and stuck his arm down her throat. With his *oosocke nauh*, he finished off that great *oochehara*,

just like that!"

She snaps her fingers. The children are oohing and aahing.

"But then... after he jumped to the ground and was just about to skin her, another *oochehara* came shuffling along, even larger. It was the husband of the first. Oh, he was a mighty bear, the king of all *oochehara*. Manteo didn't know what to do. Quickly he took his *oosocke nauh* and slit the belly of the dead one. There was an awful stink, but Manteo held his nose and crawled inside, deep inside the guts of that dead *oochehara*. He closed the flap of belly skin, leaving just a small opening where he could see out.

"Oh, it was slimy and smelly inside that carcass. The innards squished and slipped all around him. But he didn't dare move. Through the little opening, he watched the big one sniff and shuffle all around. It almost stuck its great big nose into the tiny hole. Manteo held his breath. Finally, after several moments, the great *oochehara* lumbered off and Manteo was able to come out. He was covered from head to toe with guts, but he didn't care. After he skinned the dead one, he washed in a stream nearby and covered himself up with its fur. To this day, Manteo is not afraid of the *oochehara*. To this day, when Manteo waves his *oosocke nauh*, they bow down."

She laughs and claps her hands.

"You like my story? Good, good, it is a good story."

She leaves and the children whisper excitedly among themselves. For who hasn't seen the necklace of *oochehara* claws and teeth dangling from Manteo's neck? Who could doubt such a great thing?

Chapter 35

Master Ashbury's Letter

THE *OOCHEHARA* STORY has spread like wildfire throughout the village. Manteo grunts when he hears it, but neither
confirms nor denies. The little children run up to him and
point at the necklace of teeth and claws. They clap their
hands together excitedly.

Sinopa tells the story over and over and each time she
tells it, the animals grow bigger and more ferocious. Even the
adults smile when they pass Manteo. At length, he goes to Sinopa and asks her to stop repeating such a foolish tale. The
village settles back to normal.

Not long after, I discover a letter. I've taken Regal's bridle to clean, for I wish to keep the leather supple and the
metal parts well-polished. Twisting it around in my hands, I
find a small thin piece of paper wrapped and folded, fastened
to the underside. It must have been there for a long time, for the
paper is dirty and slightly torn. Slowly I unwrap it, reading the
small fine script and hearing again Master Ashbury's voice.

My dear Jess, or Little Bird, if you prefer. A boldness within has allowed me to pen these words. I can only hope it is you who reads them. For days upon end I've walked this ship at my father's side, waiting for an opportunity to speak with you alone. When at last that opportunity came, you rejected me.

In spite of my devastation, I must only admire you. For you are courageous beyond belief. To suffer all you've suffered and still be full of hope about your future, shows great inner strength. I wish I could be part of your future, as you would be a part of mine. Perhaps one day our paths will cross again. I shall wish it so. Until then, do not forget Robert Ashbury, who adored you from afar. Your Indian is a fortunate man, indeed. Take care of Regal for me; may she have many foals to increase your herd.

Your faithful servant,
Robert Ashbury

Tears slowly run down my cheeks as I read his letter. His writings are as impassioned as any young maiden's would be. I reread the letter, then fold it carefully and place it within my amulet pouch. I'll not share it with anyone but carry it safely against my heart.

I can't get the image of Master Ashbury's letter out of my mind. I can picture him so clearly, penning the words in some obscure corner of the ship, far away from his father's prying eyes. What courage he must have had! What foolhardiness, to write so to another man's wife! What if his father had found the letter? What if my dear Akaiyan had found it and been able to read the English writing? Some small part of me cautions me to destroy his words. Some vain part of me wishes to keep them, to read and reread when the fancy strikes.

There are one or two times when I'd like to tell Mother

about Robert Ashbury and his dreams. But I don't. For Mother would sigh and wish that I'd married an English gentleman. She might ask if he'd said anything else or, perhaps, written. I couldn't lie. No, his secret passion is safe with me, tucked inside the special pouch warm against my breast.

I walk the village with a light step. For I'm home now, seeing my darling mother, my dear brother and his new wife, cherishing the *a hots*, relishing the child growing inside me. I visit Regal several times a day to stroke her, curry her, bring her special treats. Beauty whinnies low whenever she sees me, as does Star, so they have their special times also.

"Too many treats aren't good for *los caballos*," Enrique chides me. "Do you want their bellies to become fat?"

Te-lah-tai laughs, pointing at my rounding belly. I blush, then laugh with her. I know she and Enrique wish for another child, perhaps a daughter next time. I wonder how long it'll be before my brother and Sitchae announce they're to be parents. It's so hard to imagine him as a father. I remember him sitting astride the cannon on The Red Lyon calling, "Look, Jess, look, have you ever seen anything so big?"

Now he is a man. The other day he brought home a small doe slung over his shoulder. How proud he was! How we all cheered! Te-lah-tai took the animal and swiftly gutted it. Cauhau-wean skinned it and gave a generous portion to Sitchae's father. It was the proper thing to do. We had a merry feast that night.

June rounds into July. The summer sun is strong and shines down favorably on Chacandepeco. The maize grows higher and higher; our crops will be abundant this year. Akaiyan says it's because we're back home where we belong. Indeed, I think he speaks the truth.

Chapter 36

The Hunters

OUR FAR-RANGING HUNTERS report seeing many bears and, on occasion, some hostile foraging parties. The Neusiok have never traveled across the water to Croatoan. Perhaps these are Weapemeoc. Our hunters have given them a wide berth.

Summer is rounding lazily into Autumn. Already some of the leaves are turning gold. Manteo organizes two groups of men; some to fish in the deep waters, others to hunt for the furry *oochehara*. Cauhau-wean wants to go with the hunters. Akaiyan will accompany my brother and Manteo will lead that group. Master Steueens, Master Powell and some of the others will join Enrique, who prefers to try his hand at fishing. Everyone is excited about the prospect of two bountiful harvests.

The women remain at home with the children, tending the animals, gathering the crops. It's a back-breaking job to bend and pick each ear of corn, to gather the melons and the squash, to pluck the beans from the vine. Sweat pours off our faces and trickles down our backs. We envy the men, who can strip off their clothing and go about in loincloths. When no one is about, we loosen our bodices and tuck up our tunics. Some of the young girls go bare-chested, but out of deference to the English among them, the *unqua* women keep their breasts covered. I fill basket after basket, as does Te-lah-tai and the others. Sitchae works right along with the rest of us. We've become quite friendly.

Our baskets fill quickly and we sing to pass the time. I've taught the women some English nursery rhymes and other songs. They, in turn, have begun teaching me some of their lullabies and traditional songs. Our voices lift to the skies; singing makes our labor easier.

Oohahn-ne and Caun-reha come into the fields with me. I've taught Suzanne how to pluck each fat ear of corn with its plumed tassel. She's become quite good and soon her little basket is filled to the brim. William, on the other hand, can't reach the high stalks, so he gathers the long yellow squash. I laugh to watch them both.

Sinopa has told all the children about the Maize King, who lives in the corn fields and turns each tassel to silver at night. He does so when the moon is high and everyone's sleeping. With one touch of his magic *chinqua*, silver sparks fly off the end of his stick onto the cornsilk. If you peek out at night when the moon's shining, you can sometimes catch him.

Enrique's fishing group returns first, loaded down with fish. I remember when the men of Roanoak went fishing and how I had to help clean them. It was a job I never liked much and that hasn't changed. But now I do it with Suzanne watching, scaling each slippery body, trying not to look at the bulging eyes. We smoke the fish over slow-burning fires, and store them on high racks in the smoke lodge, so marauding animals can't get them.

When the men return from hunting *oochehara*, we're greatly saddened. For Manteo has been injured and Okeehah, one of the brave warriors and friend to Akaiyan, is mortally wounded. Everyone rushes to them as they're brought in. Manteo is limping on a torn leg.

"He'll need stitches," Mistress Steueens says and goes to help. At first he waves her away, then sits stoically as she sews the torn flesh together, making not a sound.

But it's Okeehah who's gravely wounded. This time the *unqua* power over the mighty *oochehara* didn't work. While trying to rescue Manteo from raking claws, Okeehah's arm is almost torn off, and great claws have sunk deep into his stomach. His *oorewa*, blanket, is soaked with blood and he grits his teeth against the pain. The men have killed two *oochehara*, but at a terrible cost.

"Will he live?" Mistress Powell asks, but Mother and Mistress Steueens shake their heads sadly.

"He's lost too much blood."

I bury my face in my hands, for the loss of so brave a warrior is too much to bear. Akaiyan is by his side. Towaye does his best but it isn't enough and we have no physician among the English. The most anyone can do is to keep him warm and offer prayers. Already, the women are keening songs of sorrow.

"My friend cannot die," Akaiyan says, his eyes bright and hard. "He is too strong to die."

"Akaiyan," I start to say, but he pulls away from me. In sorrow I go to Mother's house, there to sit and wait for the inevitable news.

Chapter 37

"The Great Spirit Knows"

THE WHOLE VILLAGE mourns its loss. When at length
Akaiyan returns from the woodlands where he spent his grieving time, his arms are cut and bloodied.

"You must eat," I say, putting the plate before him. He
just pushes it away.

"My brother was injured, too."

"Cauhau-wean?"

I nod my head. For it's true. My dear brother received
five terrible scratches on his shoulder which bled and bled.
Sitchae called for my mother and Mistress Steueens. She wept
copiously while both women ministered to him. They were
able to keep infection away. Cauhau-wean wears the scabbed
marks with great pride.

Akaiyan grunts, then puts some meat in his mouth. He
chews slowly, forcing himself to swallow.

"We'll bury him tomorrow."

The next day the sky weeps also, great drops of rain

which fall and soak us all. It's a chill rain and we stand shivering.

The burial ground is marked by totems. A large grave has been dug by the men. Manteo hobbles from his lodge house, waving away those who would assist him. Master Steueens reads from our Holy Bible.

"Our days on the earth is but a shadow, and there is none abiding...."

Manteo offers prayers, his face grey against his pain.

"*Its warke tateawa keet e chichka ahunt wackena ey whaharia*, go you far across the wide river into the land of the dead. *Ahke oosottoo eh woccanookne*, you will travel through night and darkness to be like a child again."

The prayers continue for a long time. Oohahn-ne starts whimpering, then Caun-reha and finally, all the babes.

"Take them back to the houses and change their clothing," whispers Mother, and Ooteinne and Te-lah-tai leave with the children.

Master Steueens continues reading from the Bible. The *unqua* stand there faithfully, not truly understanding but awed by his voice.

"...for earth thou art, and unto earth shalt thou return."

It is a solemn occasion, indeed, as each of us stands there remembering those we love: my dear father, young Agnes, Ananyas... oh, it is too much!

The rain beats down incessantly and the wind picks up as we leave the burial place. Akaiyan walks ahead of me alone in his sadness, rejecting my touch. But I understand. I watch them leave then follow Manteo, the last to go. I'm so glad it is not he who was killed and sense the depths of all their grief for the young brave who gave his life so freely.

"A bird falls and the Great Spirit knows," Manteo had

said a long time ago after Agnes Harvye's death. His words had washed away the tears and filled my heart with peace. Perhaps this rain is God's way of washing our pain, "...even as thou shalt know every man's heart...." I lift my face to let it fall upon me. My tears mingle with the raindrops.

The village moves in silence for days after. There's no singing at the hearth fires; even the children seem to sense the loss. Mother's shoulders seem just a little more bent; this death reminds her of all the others, especially my beloved father's. One evening, when my babe is kicking me vigorously, I take her hand and place it upon my stomach. The child within surges up. She feels its push and gives a faint smile.

"This child is anxious to be born," she whispers, her hand still pressed against me. A faint whine is heard. With her other hand, she reaches down to pet Sooka, the wolf dog. Sooka has grown from puppyhood until he's now a full adult. Though he looks like his mother, a true wolf, he's a dog in all ways. He wags his tail and pushes his nose into my mother's hand. She smiles.

"Sooka kept me company all those long months you were gone. He slept at the foot of my bed. He never left my side."

"Sweet Sooka," and I pet his head. He licks my hand. For a brief moment, my heart twists at the memory of little Che-Chou, killed by the pirates, and of Teethha, killed by Manteo himself for savaging a chicken. How I hated Manteo at that moment of Teethha's death. I'd failed to understand how much it had hurt him, too, to have to kill the little cub.

I give a great sigh and lean my head upon my mother's shoulder. She strokes my hair.

"The cycle of life moves on," she whispers. "A death, a new life, a loss, a gain...."

Chapter 38

The Link Between

PERHAPS ONE DAY Suzanne Emily, my dear Oohahn-ne, will gather together all these many sheets, this diary of my life. Perhaps she'll untie the ribbons binding them and begin to read. How will she feel?

Winter has settled like a cloak of white over the village. My new babe nurses at my breast. I've named him Wauh-kuaene. His English name is George Ananyas, after two people I loved. Suzanne and William are enchanted by him.

It's January in the year of Our Lord, 1593, and I just turned twenty last month. Mother says I should wait before I have any more children. Suzanne is almost three; William will be two in March. Te-lah-tai told me there are special potions a woman can take so she won't conceive a child. But I'm not sure. Akaiyan wants many sons and daughters; the village all help to raise the children. Sometimes Suzanne sleeps at Wenefrid Powell's house; sometimes she stays at Sinopa's. Chacandepeco reveres its children.

Suzanne's hair has turned lighter and her eyes are grey-ish green. I noticed that William's eyes are the same color. It's the same with Miguel, Enrique's little boy. His hair is lighter than any of the *unqua* and his eyes are flecked with grey. Perhaps this is what happens when they marry someone not an Indian. The intermingling of bloodlines fascinates me.

I wish there were more books to read. I've some from Mother and Father's book of poetry. Mistresses Powell and Steueens have only a few volumes between them. I've read each one. Now I've begun studying the Holy Bible. Mother says there's all of life and love in that one revered book. I'll begin at the beginning and work my way through.

The children I teach are growing before my eyes. Every day we practice our sums, our writing and reading. We've acted out little plays I've written. The children are quite good. Quayah played the part of Sinopa's Maize King, and we drew a silver moon and stars for scenery. Carlos fetched some old dried cornstalks and arranged them to look like a cornfield. The village was invited to see us perform. The entire audience stamped their feet and clapped their hands at the end.

Today it's stopped snowing and the wind has died down. I wrap my *oochehara* cloak around me and tell Mother I'm going for a walk. Te-lah-tai begs to come but I tell her no. She nods her head and turns quickly to help Mother with the children. One day, I think, Te-lah-tai may be a teacher herself. She's learning patience.

My thick furry *oo-ross-soo* make crunching sounds in the fallen snow. I find myself headed for the burial ground. It's a place that seems to draw me always. When I'm there, I feel great tranquility.

I stop first at Okeehah's totem. Akaiyan has been there already, for a large *oochehara* fur is spread over the place where he lies. It's the coat of the bear which took his life. Scattered around are several shells and beads arranged in patterns. It's Akaiyan's way of showing his feelings for his friend. Though I feel sad standing there, my soul is at peace.

"May the Great Spirit watch over you at all times. May you walk at His side and be one with Him."

A warmth floods through me from my head down to my feet. I feel as if I'm bathed in light. I fling off the *oochehara* fur and am not cold. Raising my hands to the sky, I say the only *unqua* prayer I know.

"*Oonaquera, cotuch eets hitchra waure ki-yu-se*, a thousand times may the Great Spirit give you peace."

Though my eyes are closed, I begin to see dim shapes moving toward me, coming from the mist of my mind. There is George Howe, the elder, John Tydway, little Agnes, dear Ananyas, my beloved father. They stand before me holding out their hands. I'm not afraid. For they're not calling me to enter their spirit world; rather, their love diffuses outward into me, into my very soul.

'You are blessed, dearest Jess,' says my father's voice. 'Your life is one of richness and beauty. You are the link between us and the *unqua*. Through you flows the understanding which join two groups of people.'

His voice fades and little Agnes reaches out a tentative hand.

'Remember me always,' she says in her childlike voice. Then Ananyas steps forward. How often I've dreamed of him.

'Eleanor is safe,' his voice fills my mind. 'And my child. One day, perhaps, you'll meet them again.'

They all disappear and I hear the low call of a bird, the squeak of some little animal hidden beneath the rocks and snow. I hear then the rich musical voice of Manteo and turn suddenly. It is the great chief who is standing behind me, having followed from the village. His voice is soft and there is a smile upon his face.

"Little Bird, wife of my son. He loves you so. Go and be at peace."

The mist disappears and I see only the snow upon the ground, the *oochehara* cloak spread across the earth. Leaving Manteo where he stands, I walk to my father's grave and place a lock of hair from Suzanne Emily.

Dearest Father, I think, but no tears come. For there's nothing to cry about. His spirit is at peace. Beyond this place stretches the vast wide expanse of sea, grey and white-capped. I think of all that's happened; our passage to Roanoak, our escape from the Spanish garrison. I remember the power of Elizabeth, the Queen, and her unexpected compassion. Warmth surrounds me again and I turn, walking past Manteo to go back to the village, to my children and my husband, to the *unqua* life I love so much.

Epilogue

There is no real proof that the Lost Colony intermarried with the Indians, though later settlers reported seeing Indians with blond hair and grey eyes.

As the joint-stock companies grew in power, Englishmen once again turned to the New World, planning yet more colonies. The most note-worthy of these is the Jamestown Colony of Virginia, founded in 1607.

The Indians of North America kept acquiring horses, recognizing their importance. The Indian's horse became his most valued possession.

**Read the final adventures of Jess and her
children in the fifth book of The Lyon Saga...**

The Lyon's Crown

In 1612, an English ship steams northward from Croatoan
Island. On it are Oohahne, Caun-reha and Wauh-kuaene,
otherwise known as Suzanne, William and George. The
children of Jessabel Archarde are heading for the Jamestown settlement, there to make a new life for
themselves. What will they find? And what has happened
to their parents, Jess and Akaiyan?

FURTHER READING

Daniell, David, Editor. *Tyndale's New Testament*. New Haven & London: Yale University Press, 1989.

———. *Tyndale's Old Testament*. New Haven & London: Yale University Press, 1989.

Durant, David N. *Ralegh's Lost Colony: The Story of the First English Settlement in America*. New York: Atheneum, 1981.

Hawke, David. *The Colonial Experience*. New York: Bobbs-Merrill Co. Inc., 1966.

Hoffman, Paul E. *Spain and the Roanoke Voyages*. Raleigh: North Carolina Dept. of Cultural Resources, Division of Archives and History, 1987.

Humber, John L. *Backgrounds and Preparations for the Roanoke Voyages, 1584-1590*. Raleigh: North Carolina Dept. of Cultural Resources, Division of Archives and History, 1986.

Kupperman, Karen Ordahl. *Roanoke, The Abandoned Colony*. Maryland: Rowman and Littlefield, 1984.

Lawson, John. *A New Voyage to Carolina*. Chapel Hill: University of North Carolina, 1967.

Miller, Helen Hill. *Passage to America: Ralegh's Colonists Take Ship for Roanoke*. Raleigh: North Carolina Dept. of Cultural Resources, Division of Archives and History, 1983.

Perdue, Theda. *Native Carolinians: The Indians of North Carolina*. Raleigh: North Carolina Dept. of Cultural Resources, Division of Archives and History, 1985.

Quinn, David Beers. *The Lost Colonists: Their Fortune and Probable Fate*. Raleigh: North Carolina Dept. of Cultural Resources, Division of Archives and History, 1984.

————. *Set Fair For Roanoke: Voyages and Colonies, 1584-1606*. Chapel Hill: University of North Carolina Press, 1985.

Quinn, David B. & Alison Quinn. *The First Colonists: Documents on the Planting of the First English Settlements In North America, 1584-1590*. Raleigh: North Carolina Dept. of Cultural Resources, Division of Archives and History, 1982.

Rights, Douglas L. *The American Indian in North Carolina*. Winston-Salem: John F. Blair, 1991.

Rowse, A.L. *The England of Elizabeth*. New York: MacMillan, 1961.

Singman, Jeffrey L. *Daily Life in Elizabethan England*. London: Greenwood Press, 1995.

Sitwell, Edith. *The Queens and the Hive*. Boston: Little Brown & Co., 1962.

Stick, David. *Roanoke Island: The Beginnings of English America*. Chapel Hill: University of North Carolina, 1983.

Williams, Neville. *The Sea Dogs: Privateers, Plunder and Piracy in the Elizabethan Age*. New York: MacMillan, 1975.

M.L. Stainer

Having fallen in love with North Carolina's Outer Banks, the author decided to research the early colony that once existed on Roanoke Island. What mysterious circumstances led them to disappear? The Lyon Saga books explore many possibilities as to what may have happened to those brave men, women and children. M.L. Stainer weaves fact and fiction into fascinating history. Educated in London and at Fordham University, she lives in upstate New York with her husband, Frank, and numerous dog and cat family members.

James Melvin

James Melvin always dreamed of becoming an artist. He received his formal training from North Carolina's A & T State University in 1970. For several years this degree was put to use while James served as a Peace Corps art instructor in Botswana, Africa. Presently, James lives on the Outer Banks of North Carolina where he operates Melvin's Studio and Gallery. He is well-known for his stunning portrayals of black culture and simple treasures of life. A versatile artist, he works in oils, acrylics and pastels and has illustrated more than 20 children's books. His works are owned by collectors and art lovers throughout the U.S. and abroad.